BLOOD CIRCUS

A JUNKYARD DRUID URBAN FANTASY SHORT STORY COLLECTION

M.D. MASSEY

MODERN DIGITAL PUBLISHING

CARNIVAL OF BLOOD

Note to readers: This short story takes place in the interim between *Junkyard Druid* and *Graveyard Druid*, the first and second books in the Colin McCool series. There are very few spoilers in this story, but if you haven't read *Junkyard Druid* yet, you might want to pick it up before you read *Carnival of Blood*.

"Damn it, it looks like the goblins are at it again."

Sabine and I were at a traveling carnival, enjoying the fall weather and each other's company. All afternoon, we'd been stuffing our faces with cotton candy and funnel cakes and hitting every ride in sight. While our plans for the day hadn't included carnival rides and sugar highs, I wasn't complaining.

The carnival had been set up in the empty parking lot next door to the Halloween store, where we'd been shopping for costumes and seasonal decorations. Uncle Ed and I planned to turn the junkyard into a haunted house for the annual employee party, and Sabine had offered to help with setting up props and adding in some low-level illusory magic. We had a lot to do before the day was out, but we hadn't been able to resist the temptation to check out the event.

Since the local fae queen had blackmailed me into coming out of retirement, supernatural-free afternoons like this one were rare. I hated to spoil it. Copious amounts of refined sugar, fear-fueled adrenaline, and the generally festive atmosphere of the place had Sabine in a rare, carefree form. She'd been smiling and giggling like a schoolgirl since we'd arrived, quite unlike her usual withdrawn self.

That was why, when I saw the creepy, sopping wet clown ducking behind a midway booth, I almost didn't mention it.

"Just ignore them, Colin. They're perfectly harmless."

I frowned. "Harmless? Goblins?"

"Well, mostly. The local clan hasn't eaten a human in decades. Besides, Queen Maeve decreed that they could continue scaring humans at their leisure—so long as they didn't injure anyone in the process."

"You and I both know she only said that to get them out of her hair." Goblins were nasty, dirty, deformed humanoid creatures that delighted in mischief and violence. Since Maeve had declared humans off-limits to the fae several decades ago, unseelie fae like goblins had taken umbrage with her decision. At first, she'd just had the grumblers killed—but after a decade of regular executions, her subjects had gotten restless.

So, she'd started making concessions to appease the unseelie fae in her demesne. For example, she allowed the trolls to take cattle from the surrounding countryside—so long as no one saw them doing it. Every so often, they had to make a killing look like a ritual sacrifice, or they had to leave a carcass behind for the coyotes to ravage. As far as they were concerned, that was a small price to pay for fresh, grass-fed beef. She also let household spirits—kobolds, boggarts, and the like—stage the occasional haunting.

In the case of the goblins, she let them dress up as creepy clowns so they might terrorize the local population without bringing undue attention to the fae. You would have thought the Cold Iron Circle would get involved and put a stop to it, but Maeve and the Circle had a truce. So long as a fae didn't injure or kill a human, they were off-limits.

The goblins thought it was great fun, and if it kept them

amused and off Maeve's back, it was all the better—at least as far as the queen was concerned.

Sabine tugged at my arm, dragging me in the direction of the Tilt-A-Whirl. "C'mon, Colin, forget about those creeps. Live a little! Just because Maeve tricked you into doing hunter work again, it doesn't mean every unseelie fae is your responsibility."

"Yeah, but there are kids here, Sabine. I can't just let the goblins think they can go around scaring little kids when I'm around. I do have a rep to uphold, you know."

Sabine stopped tugging on my arm and rolled her eyes. "Fine, go have your fun. And while you're chasing nasty ugly goblins, I'm going to hit the midway and win a prize."

I smirked. "Only because you're going to cheat with magic."

She held her hands up and shrugged. "Hey, if the game is rigged, how else are you going to win?"

Her chipper mood made me smile, and I considered forgetting about the clown like she'd said. But I'd been scared to death of clowns as a kid, and had suffered nightmares about them for years. I couldn't stand by and let the goblins give some poor child a nasty case of coulrophobia. Uh-uh, not on my watch.

"Have fun, Sabine. I'll catch up with you on the midway— once I convince these clowns to leave."

A slight frown flitted across her face, then it was gone. "See you in a few, druid boy."

I watched her walk away, taking a moment to enjoy the bounce in her step. Since I'd known her, my friend had dealt with feelings of low self-worth, agoraphobia, and social anxiety. And me? I'd struggled with guilt over the death of my girlfriend. Sabine and I had helped each other through our respective issues, and it was nice to see her let her hair down for a change.

"It'll only take a few minutes," I mumbled to myself. "Then I'm going to enjoy the rest of the day."

I stood in the center of the carnival as crowds of people

walked past, turning in a circle as I scanned the magical spectrum for the clown.

There. I spotted a glimmer of magic—the type that indicated a glamour. I knew it wasn't Sabine's magic by the signature, and it was in a different direction than the midway, toward the far end of the carnival.

I opened my Craneskin Bag to make sure my war club was close at hand. Chances were good the goblins would back down as soon as I threatened them with physical harm. I had recently killed a *fachen*, after all. Fachen were bad business—one-armed, one-legged giants out of Celtic lore that could flatten entire forests in a single night. So, my rep had increased dramatically once word had gotten out that I'd killed it.

It wasn't actually *me* who'd killed it, but that *other*, dark side of me. Thankfully, the goblins didn't know that. Just one look at me and my war club, and they'd think twice about scaring children at carnivals.

I pushed the sleeves up on my trench coat and headed straight for the magical signature. *Time to go to work.*

I traced the magical signature to the other end of the carnival, and soon realized why the goblins had picked that area. At the very end of the rides stood one lonely, ramshackle attraction: the fun house. Of *course* that would be where the creepy goblin clowns would set up shop. It'd be super easy to get the maximum scare effect inside a fun house, with the low lighting, confusing interior layout, mirror mazes, and so on.

But I wasn't quite sure if the clowns were actually inside there, or if they were just in the general vicinity of the place. I'd lost track of the magical signature I'd picked up earlier, which was weird. It was almost like the person casting that glamour had vanished into thin air.

I decided to hang out and do a little surveillance, just to make sure the goblins were using the fun house for their base of operations. I bought some cotton candy and sat down on a bench, nibbling at it while I kept an eye on the area. Several adults and teens went through the attraction and came out again at regular intervals, laughing and carrying on as they rode down the exit slide from the second floor.

Then, a kid walked up to the fun house. He was maybe

twelve years old and skinny, sort of goofy-looking with a slight overbite and a Cruella De Vil Mallen streak on the back of his head. He wore a Darth Vader shirt that said, "Warning: choking hazard," along with worn blue jeans and Converse high tops. The shirt made me like him immediately. I was tempted to stop him, just to share some hard-earned advice on dealing with bullies and dickheads.

Instead, I watched as he passed me by on his way to the fun house. I held back, because I remembered how awkward it had been when I was a chubby, picked-on kid and some adult tried to give me advice. Adults forget that when you're a kid, you don't believe that any adult remembers what it was like being that age. Kids see all adults as being out-of-touch, and that's a universal fact.

It happened that the kid was alone, and the only person who went in the fun house at that time. Based on what I'd observed, it took about two to three minutes to make it through the attraction. It was the size of your typical eighteen-wheeler trailer, and even with two levels, it couldn't have been bigger than a small apartment.

So, when the kid didn't come out again, I knew something was up.

I checked my watch, to get a fix on how long he'd actually been in there, and I estimated it'd been more than three minutes. I watched the exit for another two minutes, but the kid never came out. Either he'd gotten lost inside, he'd found another way out, or he was detained.

I was betting on option three. I switched over to my second sight, to check the place out in the magical spectrum—just in time to catch a brilliant burst of energy emanating from inside.

"Shit. Here we go..." I mumbled as I jumped to my feet and made a beeline for the entrance. I flashed my wristband at the ride attendant and headed inside.

The amusement ride started with a dark, confusing maze, dimly-lit by flashing black-lights that illuminated messages on the walls at regular intervals. "Beware!", "Caution!", and "Enter at Your Own Risk!" were common themes.

I switched back and forth between my normal sight and magical sight, keeping myself oriented to the dim glow of energy that remained after that initial powerful burst. I knew there was only one path to take inside the ride, but I also knew that unseelie fae were fond of casting illusions—the type that could get a person turned around if they didn't know better.

I turned a corner in the dark maze, and an animatronic clown with evil red eyes and sharp teeth popped out at me. I almost punched it in the face, breathing a sigh of relief as a tinny electronic voice cackled at me from some hidden speaker nearby. Man, I hated clowns.

A sudden movement nearby caught my attention. I turned to look, just in time to see a flash of yellow silk pants and a floppy red shoe disappear around the next turn in the maze. *Definitely a clown costume*, I thought as I chased after the fleeting figure.

The same electronic cackle I'd heard earlier echoed down the corridor ahead.

Nope, that's not creepy... at all.

I tried to put my childhood fears from my mind as I zigzagged around two more corners. No matter how quickly I moved, I couldn't catch up with the object of my pursuit. That fucking clown could run like Usain Bolt, and it pissed me off. Unfortunately, I couldn't shoot it to slow it down. For one, it might not be a goblin—and besides that, I might hit someone else in the fun house by mistake.

So, I followed the cackling laugh and the occasional flash of yellow pants and red shoes down yet another dark corridor. *If this goblin ruins McDonald's and Happy Meals for me, I'm going to be pissed*, I thought as I ran on.

Then another thought occurred to me. *Exactly how long is this fucking maze?*

Just as I began to suspect I'd gotten turned around, the maze opened up into a room. Not a single angle in the place was square and true. The floor was tilted, and the ceiling and walls were warped. A wooden butcher block table sat in the middle of the room. Tied spread eagle to the table was the kid I'd seen enter the fun house just minutes before. He was gagged with a bright yellow silk handkerchief—and based on the look in his eyes, he was frantic with fear.

I couldn't blame him, because a five-foot-nothing clown—a juggalo in whiteface, with a bright-red leering grin and a mouthful of crooked goblin teeth—stood to the side of the table. His red and yellow striped clown suit was spattered in blood, from the Tudor ruff collar at his neck to the red floppy shoes on his feet. Water dripped from his costume, where it gathered in small pools and rivulets on the cavern floor—a detail I found odd, considering it had been a clear and sunny day.

He held a long, wood-handled butcher knife in his hands. The blade was crusted with dried blood, and he worked at it furiously with a whetstone while whistling an impossibly complex calliope tune. The clown admired his work with jaundiced eyes, and he tested the edge with his thumb before gently laying a hand on the boy's shoulder.

"Sacrifice ready?" the clown asked in thickly-accented English as he carved a thin red line across the boy's cheek.

Chuckles, you just earned yourself a beatdown, I thought as I reached into my Bag.

Truth was, the sight of the clown triggered a Pandora's box full of my childhood fears. Clowns had always creeped me out, and this one was seriously giving me a case of the oh-hell-no's. So, when I strode into the room, I found myself at a loss for something suitably witty and intimidating to say.

"Hey... you!" was about all I could get out. Then I ran across the room at the juggalo goblin.

The goblin's eyes widened, and he raised the knife over his head while screaming, "Must bring clown god!" or something to that effect. It could have also been, "Mushroom cloud good!" Goblin speech was really hard to understand.

I was only halfway across the room, and the clown was about to off the kid. Lacking any alternatives, I threw my war club at the goblin's face. The club flew end over end and smacked the clown right in the teeth, sending a few flying and making him stumble. That gave me just enough time to vault over the table, landing a nice side kick to his chest.

At this point, most people would expect me to do some fancy disarm—or maybe a complicated joint-lock that would allow me to stab the clown with his own knife.

Those people would be wrong. I don't care who you are or how much kung-fu you know; facing off empty-handed against someone with a knife is scary. Hell, it's damned close to suicide if that person really wants to kill you. A knife doesn't move like a fist. It's unpredictable and can attack from any angle and still cut or stab you. I personally didn't want to see my guts spill out all over the floor, so I wisely took the time to pick up my war club.

That gave the goblin enough time to recover from my initial attack. The room wasn't that big, so he backed into a corner, brandishing that rusty, blood-stained blade at me.

"You no understand," the clown pleaded. "Child must die to bring clown god. Clown god demands blood sacrifice."

"Isn't that a little redundant, saying 'blood sacrifice'?" I asked. "That's like saying 'bō staff,' or 'true fact.' It sounds silly, and a little pretentious."

"Clown god no pretend juice!" the goblin juggalo screamed. "He have street cred, live thug life."

"Whatever, clown. All I know is that Maeve told you dumb-asses you couldn't hurt or kill humans." I pointed my club at him. "And as far as I'm concerned, you shouldn't even be near any kids in that scary-ass get-up."

"What wrong with get-up? This lifestyle, not joke. Why you throw shade?"

I rubbed the side of my face and sighed with frustration. "Look, dude, I don't care how you dress. But you can't sacrifice this kid—or any kid, for that matter—to your stupid clown god!"

"Clown god not stupid!" he yelled as he lunged at me with the knife. I sidestepped and dropped a seriously hard blow on his wrist, breaking it with a loud *snap* and causing him to drop the knife. I followed up with a forehand strike to the knee and a backhand strike to the temple. The goblin clown crumpled in a heap at my feet.

Amazingly, he was still breathing. Goblins were resilient

little shits—not quite as tough as trolls, but they were still hard to kill. I stood there looking at him for a second, considering whether or not I should end his miserable existence. A whole lot of grunting and thumping behind me reminded me why I was here.

I turned around and pulled the gag from the kid's mouth.

"Shit, man—what the hell is that dude's problem? And why is he so ugly? I thought it was just a scary clown mask, then I rubbed off some of his makeup when he was tying me up."

I pulled my hunting knife from the small of my back and began cutting the kid loose as I considered my options. This kid struck me as the curious type, the kind that got a glimpse of the world beneath and spent the rest of their life chasing the supernatural. If he'd seen what was underneath the goblin's makeup, it was going to be hard coming up with a lie that he'd accept. I needed him to trust me, so I could get him out of here safely. For expediency's sake, I decided to go with the truth. I could always get Sabine to mind-wipe him later.

"That dude is a goblin. They're all that ugly. Just be glad they don't smell like trolls."

The kid sat up and swung his legs off the side of the table. "Goblin? As in *Lord of the Rings*, D&D goblins?"

I shrugged. "Sort of. Tolkien took most of his ideas from real life supernatural creatures. Except for orcs—that shit was totally made up. What's your name, kid?"

"Well, it's not fucking kid, that's for damned sure. It's Kenny."

"Like South Park Kenny?"

He shot me a smart-assed smirk. "Ha, ha. Never heard that one before. Out of one-hundred-thousand sperm, you were really the fastest?"

"Cartman it is, then," I said matter-of-factly. "C'mon, Cartman, we need to get you out of here and back to your parents."

The kid jumped off the table. "First off, fuck you. And second, not until I find Derp."

"Who the hell is Derp?"

"Derp is about the only real friend I have in this world. No way am I going to let him get sacrificed by these insane goblin pussies."

"It's Insane Clown Posse."

"I know that—hell, I listen to ICP and know some juggalos, and these clowns are not even close. So fuck them—and fuck you if you're not going to help me. I'll find Derp myself."

Kenny started walking for the exit.

"Man, I thought I cussed a lot," I mumbled as I jumped in front of Kenny. "Look, Cartman, I didn't say I wouldn't help you. In fact, it's kind of my job."

"Got turned down for door greeter at Wal-Mart, huh?"

"Yeah... I mean, no—I'm a hunter. I hunt things like these guys."

"Buffy it is, then." The kid looked around like he was missing something. "Hey, where'd that ass-clown go?"

I looked over my shoulder. Sure enough, the goblin had disappeared, probably with the help of a glamour. A quick glance around in the magical spectrum revealed him limping toward a section of wall.

The goblin turned around and flashed a "W.C." hand sign with his arms crossed. "Whoop, whoop, bitches! Dis ninja outta here." Then, he pushed on a section of wall and slipped inside a hidden door.

I ran to the wall, but it was sealed up tight by the time I got there. "Shit. The little bastard got away."

"Hey, man, you're bleeding."

Kenny pointed at my midsection. I looked down, and he was right—my shirt was soaked. I lifted the material to reveal a nasty four-inch cut across my abdomen. I was lucky. The cut had only made it through the skin and fat, and not the muscle.

"How can you not feel that?"

"Adrenaline. Happens all the time," I said. "That's how soldiers bleed out on the battlefield. They get hit in the confusion of battle and adrenaline kicks in so they don't feel it. Adrenaline causes vasoconstriction, so even though your heart is pumping faster, you don't bleed as much at first. Later, when it wears off, that's when your blood pressure drops and you pass out..."

Kenny covered his eyes with his hand and groaned, cutting me off. "You can stop right there, Dr. Google. Next time skip the science channel soundbites and just say, 'adrenaline.' I might be a kid, but I have the Internet, too."

I rustled around in my Craneskin Bag for a first-aid kit. "I'm starting to think I should've just let the goblin kill you, Kenny."

Kenny hopped back up on the table while he watched me patch myself up. "Yeah, yeah, I've heard it all before. Smart-ass is my default setting, so get used to it. And anyway, you aren't exactly the world's least sarcastic person either. I bet you piss off a ton of people with that pissy fucking personality of yours."

"Alright, already—enough with the f-bombs."

Kenny flipped me off. "Like you never cussed when you were a kid. Every kid cusses. It's like a rite of passage or something."

I grabbed a first-aid kit from my Craneskin Bag, then cleaned the wound and sprinkled a clotting agent on it to stop the bleeding. "If I'd cussed like you, Cartman, I'd have slipped up eventually and gotten my mouth washed out with soap—*A Christmas Story*-style."

"Been there, done that. It's not so bad. That Ralphie kid was kind of a pussy. Who cries when they're beating someone's ass? If I was stomping a bully's head into the ground, I'd be smiling."

I applied a piece of gauze and taped the wound up tight. Then I swept a hand grandly in Kenny's direction. "Ladies and gentlemen, the future of our nation."

"Damn straight. And when you're in the old folks' home, I'll be dating your much younger wife."

"I'm, like, ten years older than you. And I date women my own age."

Kenny smirked. "Sure you do, right now. But your generation is running from manhood. You guys just want to watch porn and play video games all day. No way you're getting married until you're in your sixties. Then, it'll be to some wide-eyed coed who thinks your dad bod is sexy."

He was a smart kid—probably smart enough to attract regular ass-beatings from bullies. He reminded me of myself at his age.

"I am not having this conversation with you, Cartman. Now, let's go." I approached the wall the goblin had disappeared into, and began tapping on it with my club.

"Whatever, Buffy. Hey, you got a sword in that bag? Can I have one?"

"No, Kenny, you can't have a sword. And how would I fit a sword in this bag?"

Kenny crossed his arms. "Oh, quit fucking around already. If goblins really exist, then that's a bag of holding if I ever saw one. You stuck your arm into it almost up to the shoulder. If you're trying to keep it a secret, you might want to be a bit subtler the next time you pull a baseball bat out of your man purse."

"It's not a... never mind. Stand back, I'm going to bust us an exit." I reared back and swung at the wall, just as hard as I could. The plywood barrier exploded into splinters.

Kenny was beside himself with glee at the destruction my club had wrought. "Holy shit! Man, you gotta give me one of those."

"Sorry, it's the only one." I stuck my head through the hole, muttering a spell to enhance my vision. "Damn, this doesn't bode well for us."

"*Bode*? Who talks like that? You're a bigger dork than me and Derp put together." Kenny elbowed his way past me. "Lemme see."

I pulled him back, just as he was about to fall into the vast, empty void beyond the wall.

"Shit, man! Why didn't you warn me?" he exclaimed.

"Because you didn't think to ask."

"Asshat."

"Shit biscuit."

"That doesn't even make sense."

I looked out the hole one more time, verifying what I'd seen the first time. There were definitely things moving around out there in that void—huge, eldritch, otherworldly things that defied description. An enormous gaping mouth in a clump of tentacles, filled with row after row of teeth that spun like a pinwheel. A cuboid creature made of fire and smoke and blood. A giant tree-man that floated in the nothing, walking step by step through the void, somehow managing locomotion in empty space.

"Fuck." I said it and immediately regretted it. "Help me move that table in front of this hole."

"But that's where the clown went. How're we going to follow him if we don't use the same door?"

"That's not where he went. He stepped through a teleportation portal, and whoever or whatever created it closed it immediately after." I pointed at the hole in the wall. "That out there is another dimension, maybe one of the planes of Hell, or some empty Void where shit straight out of Lovecraft's warped mind lives. Do I have any idea why part of this funhouse resides in another dimension? Nope. But if we don't close that hole up, something way more wicked and nasty than that clown is going to come through. And frankly, I'm not trained to handle that kind of shit-show."

We moved the table to the wall and flipped it over. Then, I grabbed some silver spikes from the Bag and used my club to hammer them into the wall through the table. I hoped they'd be enough to hold it. I could've warded the damned thing, but I didn't think anything I could cast would be enough to keep one of those things out. Besides, the magic would glow like a beacon out there, drawing unwanted attention from the Old Ones or whatever the hell those things were.

We rested for a moment after I was done. Then we tried to backtrack, just to see if we could. Unfortunately, we ended up right back in the room with the hole in the wall that led to the nightmare dimension.

"Something really powerful and really twisted is screwing with us," I mumbled.

"No shit, Sherlock. Now what?" Kenny asked.

"Now, we keep going through the fun house. Hopefully, we'll run into your friend and get the hell out in one piece."

5

Kenny and I headed out the door opposite from the one I'd entered minutes prior. Strangely, the interior scale of the fun house corridors expanded the farther along we went. The nature of the walls, floor, and ceiling changed as well, transforming gradually from cramped plywood hallways to large stone passages. Oddly enough, black-light bulbs above and lighted arrow signs mounted on the walls continued to light our way. Apparently, someone had also turned on the fog machine, because the floors soon became obscured by thick mists that clung to our legs as we passed.

"I don't think we're in Kansas anymore, Toto," Kenny muttered.

I glanced over at him, noting the way his eyes were darting around. A high, chilling laugh echoed from the corridor ahead, and the kid nearly jumped out of his shoes.

"Hang on a second." I stuck my arm out to stop him, keeping him behind me as I scanned the cavernous passageway ahead. "Alright, I think we're good. Kenny, do you know how to shoot?"

He gave a half-shrug. "I've played a lot of first-person shooters. Does that count?"

"Ever play any arcade shooting games?"

"At the theater, sure. They always have some old-ass arcade games in the lobby."

I nodded and pulled a Glock 9mm from my bag. "Good deal. Listen, I'm trusting you with this, because I want you to be able to protect yourself. But you have to understand it's not a toy."

"Yeah, yeah—don't shoot you, I get it."

I sucked air through my teeth, wondering if this was such a good idea. I decided I wouldn't feel right if I left the kid completely helpless, and if we got separated he'd need a way to defend himself. So, I gave him a crash course in Glock 101.

"Okay, check it out. The magazine holds seventeen rounds, plus there's one in the chamber—so there's no need to rack the slide." I press-checked the chamber and dropped the slide, showing him what I was doing. "Glocks don't have an external safety, which means if you pull the trigger it's going to go *boom*, every damned time. Keep your finger off the trigger, and keep the muzzle pointed away from us both. Grip it with both hands, like this. If you have to shoot, take your time. Line up a good sight picture, aim for center mass—right in the middle of their chest—and gently squeeze the trigger twice."

I put the pistol back in my concealment holster and handed it to him. "Tuck it inside your belt, and keep it holstered unless you're in danger. And I'm getting that back when we're out of here. Got it?"

He looked me in the eye and pursed his lips, then nodded. "Got it."

I waited to see if he needed help clipping the holster to his belt. He didn't. He also didn't make the stupid mistake of placing the holster where he couldn't easily reach it. *Smart kid.* I pulled out my Kahr subcompact 9mm from my Bag, and holstered it in similar fashion. It was a lot smaller than the Glock, but contrary to popular belief, the larger weapon would be easier for smaller hands to control.

"We're obviously not inside the carnival fun house anymore, so there's no telling what's up ahead. Keep that pistol holstered until I say so. And if we get separated, shoot first and ask questions later. Let's go."

I headed up the corridor again, taking my time and listening carefully for signs of danger or pursuers. Outside the occasional sinister laugh, and the *plip-plop* of condensation falling from the ceiling above, it was deathly quiet.

And that made me nervous.

After a few minutes of cautiously creeping down the tunnel, the corridor widened out into a large, cavernous chamber—maybe two hundred feet across. Halfway across the chamber, waves lapped at the shore of a small underground lake. A row of gondola-style boats, like the kind found in old-school "tunnel of love" amusement attractions, sat half in and half out of the water, their tail ends lodged in the dark sand of the subterranean lakeshore.

"Why do I feel like we're about to get jumped by the Falmer?" Kenny asked.

"Yeah, I'm getting a definite dungeon crawl vibe here." I cast a night-vision cantrip and looked around the cavern, searching for exits. It looked as though the lake drained into a cavern across the way. "Seems as though the only way out of here is across the lake. We're going to be exposed when we cross this chamber, so stick close to me, alright?"

Kenny gulped and nodded. I stayed low to reduce my silhouette, and began slinking across the cavern toward the dark, sandy beach ahead. We were halfway to the boats when Kenny tugged on my sleeve.

"What is it? Do you need to pee? Because now would be a good time, before we get in one of those boats."

Kenny shook his head slowly, his eyes widening. Then, he raised one small finger and pointed overhead. I looked up, and nearly shit my pants.

Thick, cable-like spiderwebs covered the ceiling in a vast network of translucent ropy strands. Each strand of webbing glistened in the pale light, as if covered by something wet and goopy. I had no doubt that if we touched one of those lengths of web, we'd be held fast.

Of course, scattered throughout the web were at least a dozen giant spiders—large black and yellow arachnids with bodies five or six feet in length, and leg spans easily three times that.

And all of them had their beady little eyes fixated on us.

"You have to be flipping kidding me. Run for the boats, Kenny!"

6

As soon as we bolted for the shoreline, the spiders began dropping from the ceiling. I tossed my war club in my Bag, and grabbed a wicked little Celtic-style short sword instead. The club was great for bashing in fae, and it did have better reach. But if one of those spiders spat or shat their webbing at me, I damned sure wanted at least half a chance at cutting myself loose.

Kenny was right on my heels as we ran. I skidded to a stop as a spider landed in front of us, cutting us off from the boats. The damned thing came at me, clicking its fangs together. I pulled a Sam Gamgee, sliding under those fangs as I stabbed that fucker right in the baby maker. It was mean as hell, but the bitch had it coming.

I rolled out from under Shelob's little sister, slicing two of its legs off as I stood. It was already dead, it just didn't know it yet—and it was fighting to its last breath to kill me. It spun toward me, snagging me with its forelegs and pulling me toward its fangs, which dripped with venom. I stabbed it in the head, right between both rows of its beady little eyes. The spider collapsed and released me, and I kicked it off to gain space to maneuver.

Three shots rang out to my left. Kenny had decided it was open season on giant spiders, and damn it if the kid wasn't a halfway decent shot. He'd plugged a couple of the things, although the 9mm hollow points weren't having much effect. A .44 magnum or 10mm would have been a better choice for bear-sized spiders, but at least they were keeping their distance from him.

But the spiders were trying to flank him, and when they did he'd be their snack. I charged the one closest to me, jumping on its back and plunging my short sword into the joint between its head and thorax. This sword was made for stabbing, and it slid in easily to the hilt. The spider staggered a few steps, and I hung on to the hilt for dear life until the beast crashed to the cave floor.

Kenny was alternating shots between the other two, keeping them back. But more were coming from the entrance side of the cavern, and I knew that soon we'd be overrun.

"Kenny, head for the boat, now!"

He glanced over his shoulder. "Which boat?"

"I don't know, pick your favorite color. Now, run!"

He fired a couple more shots, then did as I asked. I jumped off the dead spider's back, sprinting to get myself between Kenny and the other two spiders. As I did, I reached into my Bag for one of my jury-rigged spells—an M-80 firecracker enhanced with minor spell work and runes drawn on with a permanent marker. I cast a small cantrip to light the wick, then tossed it between the spiders and took off at a dead sprint for the boats.

The magic bomb went off like a thunderclap, stunning the two spiders. Without any projectiles glued to the outside, it was nothing more than a homemade flashbang bomb, but that was all we needed. The spiders backed away from the noise and flash, giving me enough time to reach the boat Kenny had selected.

Kenny was fumbling with a guy rope when I caught up to him. I slashed it in two and drove my shoulder into the boat's stern.

"Pink? Your favorite color is pink?" I yelled as I strained against the fuchsia hull.

"It looked purple to me, fuckwad. What can I say, I like Prince!"

Kenny threw the remains of the rope into the ship and jumped in, drawing the pistol again and leaning over the starboard side to shoot at the rapidly advancing spiders. I finally got the boat in the water, splashing through the shallows for several more feet as I struggled to get us well out into the lake. I prayed there wasn't anything worse than the spiders under its surface. Once the water reached my waist, I jumped into the boat.

My chest heaved from the exertion of the battle, but we needed to get farther from the shore. As I recalled, some spiders could swim and even walk on water, using the surface tension to their advantage. I doubted that natural physics would allow an eight-hundred-pound spider to walk on water, but I also had no idea if those fuckers could hold their breath. So, I grabbed the pole from the bottom of the boat and started poling us away from shore. Kenny was still taking pot-shots at the spiders on the beach behind us.

"Stop shooting," I ordered. "We may need the ammo later."

He complied, holstering the weapon with a snorting laugh, one that soon turned into hysterical laughter. Soon the kid was rolling around in the bottom of the boat, and I worried he was losing it.

"Dude, are you alright?"

Kenny sat up, wiping his eyes and stifling a few giggles. "Yeah, I'm fine. We're about to get eaten by a herd of giant freaking spiders, and you're worried about riding in a pink boat. Wow, do you have gender identity issues or what?"

I kept poling us out into the middle of the lake, toward the exit tunnel, checking the ceiling above us to ensure no spiders were about to drop down on us. "Technically, a group of spiders is known as a cluster, not a herd. And I'm quite secure in my manhood, thank you very much."

Kenny looked over his shoulder at the spiders on the shore one last time, then cast me a sideways glance and smirked. "You are such a walking penile erection. But you saved my ass, for sure—so I'm going to cut you a break."

"Gee, thanks, Captain Shit-crumb." Just as he opened his mouth to deliver a scathing reply, I stopped him cold. "By the way, good shooting back there."

Kenny squinted at me, then leaned back against the starboard gunwale and kicked his feet up on the other side. "Meh, I guess you're alright. For a dick-diddling ass-munch, that is."

"So, how'd you get powers and stuff?"

Kenny was sitting in the front of the boat, chomping on an energy bar I'd given him from my Bag while I poled the boat down the tunnel. There was a slight current, so the going had been easy thus far. All I had to do was keep the boat from crashing into the walls... and duck to avoid the occasional trap.

Earlier, I'd nearly been decapitated by a huge circular saw blade that had swung out from the wall. Other traps had included a giant wooden sledge hammer, a Swiss ball-sized boxing glove on a spring-loaded arm, and an animatronic clown holding a fire hose that was actually a flamethrower.

"I don't know what you're talking about," I replied as I scanned the walls and ceiling ahead.

"Oh, come on. Seriously? So far, we've run into a goblin obsessed with summoning some crazy clown god, and giant cave spiders. You keep wiggling your fingers and mumbling under your breath in a foreign language that I don't recognize. It's gotta be magic, right? Then there's the fighting—you really do remind me of Buffy, you know that?"

"Not Angel or Spike?"

"Naw, man, they're monsters." He paused and narrowed his eyes. "You're not a monster, are you?"

"Nope, completely human." *Almost, anyway.* "I'm what some call a 'born champion.' Maybe one in a thousand humans are born with peak-human abilities, and the theory is that we were created—or that we evolved—as a way to balance the scales between our species and supernatural predators."

"Hah! So you are Buffy."

"More or less."

"Cool." Kenny scratched his head. "One in a thousand is a lot. Why haven't I run into one of these champions before?"

"Because supernatural creatures are drawn to us, like moths to a flame. Except usually it's the would-be human champion who gets burned. The first brush a champion has with the supernatural almost always ends up being fatal. Trust me, it may sound cool to have abilities beyond that of a normal human, but it's a major pain in the ass most of the time."

"Like how?"

"For example, when I was just a few years older than you, an ancient fae vampire tried to kill me because he had a grudge against my family."

"What's a fae?" Kenny asked.

"The more common term is 'fairy,' although they're anything but something out of a modern fairy tale. Fae typically lack any sort of empathy whatsoever—in fact, most of the ones I've met are complete sociopaths. Some fae look like elves from fiction and legend, beautiful and deadly. Others are much less refined, like the goblin you ran into earlier. And a few are completely monstrous, powerful and frightening beyond your worst nightmares."

"Worse than those giant spiders?"

"Way worse."

Kenny stood up quickly, nearly capsizing the boat. "Holy

crap... you're telling me it's real, all of it? Bigfoot, zombies, the Loch Ness Monster, vampires, werewolves, mummies, and all that other stuff?"

"Bigfoot and zombies are debatable. But yeah, the rest is pretty much real—and that's the problem. I've had nothing but trouble with the fae and other supernaturals since that vampire came after me. If I had my way, I'd have never found out that fae and monsters are real."

Kenny sat up and turned to face me. "You're kidding, right? We totally kicked ass against those spiders back there. Sure, I was scared shitless, but this is the most fun I've had in like, ever. How could you *not* like fighting monsters for a living?"

"I never said I did it for a living—although sometimes I do get paid for it. But mostly, I get sucked into a scheme some semi-immortal creature has cooked up—and almost always against my will. Right now, the local queen of the fae is blackmailing me to be her errand boy—which really sucks because I hate those pricks. And besides that, people die doing this work. A lot."

Kenny rubbed his forehead with his palm. "Who died? Someone close to you? It must be, the way you're all bitter and cynical and stuff."

I considered whether or not I wanted to get into my personal issues with a twelve-year-old kid I'd just met. But I could tell where this was headed for Kenny, and if I could discourage him from pursuing the supernatural further, I would.

"My girlfriend. Trust me, I know what you're thinking. You just found out about this crazy world that exists just beneath our own—a world where monsters are real and where you can fight them like a real-life video game. But the thing is, in real life you don't get multiple lives. You don't get to reload your last checkpoint or save. You make one mistake, and that's it. You're a goner. Or you get someone else killed, and then you have to live with it for the rest of your life.

"Believe me when I say there's no upside to this life. You can't tell anyone what you do, because that would just draw them into your world and potentially put them in danger. Or they'd try to have you committed. It doesn't always pay the greatest, and it's hard to hold down a regular job when you're out hunting monsters into the wee hours every night. And you're always looking over your shoulder. Always.

"Do yourself a favor, kid. After we find your friend and get out of here, when this is all over, just forget it ever happened. If you're lucky, this will be your only brush with the supernatural world, and you'll get to live out the rest of your life as a normal person. Goodness knows I wish I could."

Kenny crossed his arms. "I'll think about it. But shit, man, how the hell can anyone just go back to their old life once they find out all that stuff is real?"

I poled us down the tunnel toward a pinpoint of light up ahead. "That, my man, is a very good question. But if you value your life and the lives of the people you care about, that is exactly what you'll do."

8

As we neared the end of the tunnel it opened up slightly, and the current became slightly stronger. A huge, arrow-shaped, lighted sign ahead pointed to another cave opening, with "EXIT!" spelled out in flashing, multi-colored bulbs. The current seemed to be taking us toward that opening, and the closer we got, the faster we went.

"Something's not right here," I said.

Kenny cocked his head and held a hand up to his ear. "Hey, do you hear that? It sounds like the ocean or something."

I focused in on what my ears were telling me, instead of what I was seeing. "Shit. That's not the ocean. It's a waterfall." I looked around frantically for a means of escape. All I saw were smooth stone walls to the left and right, but if the goblins used this waterway then there had to be another exit nearby. As we sped toward the exit and our premature demise, I switched to my second sight and looked at the walls again.

There.

"Kenny, get ready to jump."

"Jump where?"

"Just trust me, okay? When I say go, jump at that wall like

your life depends on it." I helped him balance near the starboard gunwale. "Get ready. Wait, wait... jump, now!"

Kenny gave me a look that said if he died it would be my fault, then he jumped for the wall, disappearing through it. I jumped right after, landing in an awkward heap on top of him.

"Ow! Damn, Buffy, you need to go on a diet."

The roar of the waterfall filled the small side tunnel we'd landed in. I disentangled myself from the kid and stood, then stuck my head back through the illusion—just in time to watch our boat pass beneath the flashing exit sign to its doom.

Well, at least we dodged that bullet. Shit.

I pulled back and helped Kenny to his feet. "You alright?"

He rubbed the side of his torso and winced. "I think you broke my ribs, you moose. Geez, give me a second."

Kenny leaned against the wall of the narrow passage, kneading his ribs and giving me dirty looks. I decided to scout ahead while he recovered, noting that the passage continued ahead at a slight incline. It was unlit, but I could see light where the tunnel ended, approximately fifty feet ahead.

When I returned from my brief scouting expedition, Kenny pushed off the wall with a groan.

"Anything broken?" I asked.

He shook his head. "I don't think so. How'd you know there was a tunnel hidden there?"

"I guessed."

"Seriously? You bet our lives on a guess?"

I chuckled. "No, you goof. I knew there had to be an exit somewhere, so when I couldn't see one I scanned the area in the magical spectrum."

"Huh?"

I wiggled my fingers in the air in front of his face. "Magical powers. I can 'see' magic—not with my eyes, but in my mind's eye with my second sight. It's one of the first things you learn to do when you study magic."

Kenny's face grew thoughtful. "Can anyone learn how to do that?"

"Sure, if you have the talent." I stood silent for a moment, just looking at him. "Didn't anything I said earlier sink in with you?"

"Yeah, yeah—the supernatural world is dangerous, leave it alone, blah, blah, blah. Didn't thirty years of 'say no to drugs' teach adults anything? You tell a kid that something is bad or dangerous, and what's the first thing they're going to do? Duh, they're going to go check it out, that's what."

My shirt felt warm and wet, so I checked my wound; it was bleeding again. I was definitely going to need stitches. "Well, it's your funeral. Don't say I didn't warn you."

Kenny flipped me off.

"On that note, let's go find your friend so we can get the hell out of here and never see each other again."

The kid rolled his eyes, crossed his arms, and looked away. "Whatever."

I let him sulk and headed up the tunnel. As the roar of the waterfall faded behind us, new sounds echoed through the small passage, giving us a hint of what was ahead. We heard a bunch of what I assumed were goblins, chanting something about a clown god rising from the circus clown underworld—or something to that effect. Steady, booming drum beats punctuated the chants.

We snuck to the end of the tunnel, crawling the last few feet on our bellies. The tunnel exited on a sort of balcony ledge, roughly thirty feet above a vast circular chamber. The ledge followed the chamber wall around both sides, until it met on the side opposite us at a staircase that led down to the floor of the chamber. Beneath us, dozens of goblins dressed as clowns danced around an altar, stomping their feet and waving various bladed weapons as they chanted in a prosodic rhythm. Two drummers beat large hollow logs with the femur bones of some huge animal or creature.

And at the center of it all, tied on the altar, was a chubby blond-headed kid about Kenny's age.

"Chants and drumming. That's not cliché at all," I quipped. I pointed at the altar. "The illustrious Derp, I presume?"

9

Kenny nodded, eyes narrow and a grim look of determination on his face. He began to stand as he reached for the pistol I'd loaned him. I quickly grabbed his arm and pulled him back down before he was noticed.

"Whoa there, sport... not so fast. We need a plan."

"They're about to sacrifice Derp!"

"I can see that, but if you haven't noticed, we're outnumbered about twenty to one. We need to either cause a distraction, so you can free Derp and sneak him out while I hold them off, or we need to take them all out at once."

"Can't you just blast them with fireballs or magic lightning or something?"

I shook my head. "A better magician or druid could, but I'm just not that good at magic."

Kenny snorted. "Some magician you are. Can't you at least cast an illusion, to get their attention or scare them off?"

I snapped my fingers. "That's it! Ever see *The Princess Bride*?"

"Duh. Do you have a holocaust cloak and a wheelbarrow in that bag?"

"Nope, but I have something better. Look, I'm going to distract the goblins from up here, and when I do, I need you to be in position on the other side of this chamber. As soon as the goblins are looking at me, you're going to cut Derp loose and make a run for it. Got it?"

He nodded. "Yeah, I can do that. But what about you?"

"If my plan goes well, I'll scare the goblins away and we'll all get the hell out of here alive."

"And if not?"

"It was nice knowing you, kid."

Kenny scratched behind his ear. "You are such a dork. Everything that comes out of your mouth sounds like a line from an eighties action movie."

"Cartman, what a lovely, heartfelt sentiment. I'm touched."

"See what I mean? Don't get yourself killed, nerd, because I may not be able to find my way out of here alone." He took off before I could reply, scrambling around the edge of the chamber at a low crawl.

I had to admit, the kid was growing on me.

I opened my Craneskin Bag and shifted through all the crap Sabine and I had picked out at the Halloween store, looking through the masks and outfits to find the one I wanted: Pennywise, the clown from Stephen King's *IT*.

"Man, if I'm too late and these assholes actually manage to summon something like Pennywise or Vermoud the Clown God of Destruction, I'm might just shit my pants," I muttered to myself, searching for more supplies.

Within minutes, I'd put together a reasonably believable costume, which consisted of the Pennywise outfit, lots of fake blood, and my real sword and war club—just in case. I also had some magically-enhanced smoke bombs and M-80s scattered on the floor around me, which I intended to use for special effects. I set my tactical flashlight on strobe, propping it up so it pointed at the wall behind me. As I stood, I cast a cantrip to amplify my voice.

"WHO DARES SUMMON ME INTO THEIR PRESENCE?" I shouted in the deepest, most intimidating voice I could muster. My words echoed across the chamber, and I muttered the cantrip to light the smoke bombs.

The drumming and chanting below stopped, and the goblins turned their eyes up to the balcony where I stood. They began muttering and arguing amongst themselves, trying to decide whether or not I was the real clown god.

"COME CLOSER, MY CHILDREN, SO I CAN SEE WHO WISHES TO SERVE ME."

A few goblins began to shuffle my way, then more followed. Soon, the entire goblin clan was assembled below me. I waited to speak until Kenny had cut Derp loose and snuck out the tunnel we'd entered through. I tried to get his attention by surreptitiously motioning at another exit tunnel, but my antics drew odd stares from the goblins at ground level. *Shit.*

"PROSTRATE YOURSELVES IN MY PRESENCE!" I yelled suddenly.

The goblins looked at each other in confusion, and one or two stuck their hands down the back of their clown pants.

"NO, I MEANT... OH, NEVER MIND. KNEEL, FOOLS!"

Several of the goblin clowns nodded in understanding, and they dropped to their knees while doing the "I'm not worthy" bow, over and over. Others soon followed, but one goblin remained unconvinced—the one Kenny and I had run into when we'd first entered the fun house. His clothes had dried somewhat, but it was the same clown. He stood there, arms crossed, rubbing his chin and eyeballing me. I decided I'd better head his dissent off at the pass, before he turned the tables.

"WHO DARES TO STAND IN THE PRESENCE OF THE CLOWN GOD?"

The other goblins turned, as if I'd just said, "Who does not want to wear the ribbon?" They started muttering, and a few looked like they were about to attack the lone unbeliever.

Then the turd pointed up at the club in my hand and began to open his mouth. I beat him to the punch, drowning his words out, because I knew what he was about to say. He'd recognized my voice, and the club had cinched it for him.

"THE UNBELIEVER MUST BE PUNISHED! LOOK, I HAVE ALREADY PAINTED MY FACE WITH YOUR FIRST SACRIFICE, AND NOW I DEMAND THAT YOU SACRIFICE THIS BLASPHEMER AS WELL!"

The goblins looked at each other in confusion once more, scratching their heads and mumbling as they discussed the meaning of blasphemer.

"GAH... GRAB THE GOBLIN WHO REFUSES TO KNEEL —KILL FOR YOUR CLOWN GOD!"

That got them moving. The lone goblin clown who knew it was a lie began to back away as he yelled frantically. "Homie's an imposter! Not real clown god—a fake, a fake!"

But the other goblins' chants of "Kill for the clown god!" drowned out his yells, and soon the rest of his clan had tied him up on the altar. Before I knew it, they were stabbing the clown goblin, over and over, until his blood ran in rivers down the altar.

That would have been a good thing—except that, as the goblin's blood began to seep into the cracks in the floor below, the ground began to shake and rumble. The goblins began to back away from the altar. As they did, the floor cracked open and swallowed the sacrifice up, altar and all. As the altar sank into the darkness below, a portal opened in the empty space that was left, swirling in a rainbow kaleidoscope of circus lights and blood.

The real clown god was coming, in answer to the very real sacrifice I'd just insisted upon. *Gulp.*

The goblins milled around in confusion, looking up at me and back at the portal in front of them. An enormous, red-gloved hand reached over the edge of the portal, attached to a pale-white wrist. I estimated that whoever or whatever that hand belonged to must have easily been thirty feet tall, and I didn't care to stick around to find out if I was right.

"UM... TIME FOR ME TO GO. UH, THANKS FOR THE LOVELY SACRIFICE. YOUR EFFORTS ARE APPRECIATED, AND... BE SURE TO DONATE TO THE SHRINER'S HOSPITAL!"

I ducked back into the cloud of smoke and headed for the exit that Kenny and Derp had taken.

10

I ran to the end of the tunnel, catching up with the two boys in seconds. They had their heads sticking through the illusion, so I pulled them back through. Both boys jumped and screamed. I realized I was still wearing the scary clown mask, and pulled it off.

"Oh, it's just Buffy." Kenny sighed. "Shit, you gave me a heart attack."

"You know this guy?" Derp asked his friend. Kenny nodded, and Derp turned on me. "What the hell is wrong with you, man? You nearly made me piss myself, and I just got these pants yesterday."

Kenny rolled his eyes. "Seriously, Derp? All your clothes come from yard sales and the thrift store. Like anyone is going to notice a few piss stains."

Derp punched Kenny in the arm. "These were nearly new when I got them, asshat. At least until you let me go into the fun house by myself. Fuck! I was in the hall of mirrors when that weird-ass clown grabbed me, tied me up, and dragged me all over the place—and now, look... they're ruined."

Kenny rubbed his arm. "Alright, already. I'll buy you another pair. Sheesh."

I cleared my throat. "Um, boys? We have bigger worries right now. For one, about three dozen angry goblin clowns are about to come storming down that tunnel. And second, I think I—uh, well... I think I actually summoned the clown god."

"You *what*?" Kenny yelled. "How?"

"Is he angry—or hungry?" Derp squeaked.

I looked at both boys. "Probably both, but I'll have to explain how it happened later. Did you see any other way out of here?"

They shook their heads. "Nope, none. Just the waterfall of doom," Kenny replied. "Can't we just go back and find another way out?"

The sounds of dozens of footsteps answered his question, followed by chants of "Kill the imposter god!"

Derp's eyes grew wide. "I guess that answers *that* question."

I stuck my head through the illusion into the tunnel of love, and looked everywhere for a solution. There really was no other way out but over the waterfall, but for some reason my eyes were drawn to the flashing "EXIT" sign pointing at the tunnel's terminus. I thought back to the dripping wet clown who had been sacrificed to summon the clown god, just moments before.

Could it be? Only one way to find out.

I hope I'm right about this, I thought to myself.

"Boys, I've got good news and bad news," I said.

Kenny glanced over my shoulder and up the tunnel. "They're coming, and they look pissed. Quit fucking around and just tell us how to get out of here, Buffy!"

"Good news is that I know how to get out of here. The bad news is this." I grabbed both boys by their shirt collars and tossed them through the illusion, into the rapids of the tunnel of love on the other side. Then, I took one last look over my shoulder and followed after.

We landed in the water with three distinct splashes, one right after the other. Kenny had managed to snag the edge of the cave wall as I tossed him, so that caused him to land just after his pal. The current immediately began dragging us toward the roar of the waterfall at the end of the tunnel. Kenny and Derp both swam against the current with all their might, but it was no use.

"Don't fight it—just go with it. Trust me!" I yelled. My reassurances turned out to be unnecessary, as they both got swept away.

They disappeared over the ledge, each screaming in fear and anger. I let myself be dragged over as well, and fell off the waterfall into darkness below, spinning end over end in ragdoll fashion.

How far we fell, I had no idea. But seconds later, I landed on a hard, unforgiving surface. I sat up and shook my head, and saw that we were just inside the exit to the fun house. A beaded curtain swayed in the wind next to us, and beyond I could see the lights of the midway shutting down, one by one. It was dark outside, and stars twinkled in the blackness above.

If my clothing hadn't been soaked through, and if Kenny and Derp hadn't been looking back at me dumbfounded, I'd have thought it all a dream. I sat for a moment, stunned... then remembered what sort of danger we were in. I leapt to my feet and dragged them with me.

"We have to get out of here—like now," I said.

"You don't have to tell me twice," Kenny grumbled.

"I second the motion," Derp said.

I watched as the boys headed through the curtain and down the exit chute, their wet clothing making squeaking sounds on the hard yellow plastic of the slide as they descended. I paused inside the door of the fun house, rustling around in my Bag for what I needed.

I pulled out a can of lighter fluid and a pack of matches, and doused the hallway liberally with the fluid. The pungent odor of petroleum distillates filled the hall, and I stepped back and lit the entire pack of matches—just as the first goblin clown appeared in midair, plopping down on the floor a few feet away.

I tossed the matches into the lighter fluid and watched as the walls, floor, and ceiling between myself and the goblin lit up in flames. The goblin backed away from the heat, and I gave a smart-assed salute as I turned and headed out the door.

11

M inutes later, the boys and I sat at a nearby Whataburger, chowing down and shivering in the air-conditioned dining room. Whataburger dining rooms were always kept just this side of freezing, no matter what time of year it was. I think it was a corporate edict or something.

Derp dipped a fry into his chocolate shake. He stared at it for several long seconds before popping it into his mouth, chewing in silence with a faraway look in his eyes. Since we'd rescued him, the kid had proven worthy of his nickname several times, and Kenny razzed him constantly for it. Derp seemed to take it in stride, and gave as good as he got. But beneath the goofiness and adolescent hijinks, it was easy to see he was in shock after the events of the evening.

Kenny, on the other hand, was beside himself with excitement. He'd been chattering and asking questions about the world beneath nonstop since we'd escaped the fun house. Based on past experience, I knew that level of curiosity about the supernatural would not end well for the boy—not at all.

The truth was, I worried about their sanity and future, should they decide to keep messing around with the supernatural. While Derp ate and Kenny chattered, I started working on an excuse to slip away for a few moments, so I could call Sabine and get her to mind-wipe them both.

"I still can't believe you set the thing on fire," Kenny said, shaking his head.

I held a finger up to my lips. "Shhh! Someone might hear and connect us to the incident." I took a drink of sweet tea with a loud slurping noise, shaking the cup to get at the last few drops before I set it on the table. "Besides, I couldn't let that clown god thing come through, whatever it was. As it stands, it's probably caught between our world and its own now. I'd bet dimes to donuts that we haven't seen the last of it."

Kenny pushed a French fry around in a container of ketchup. "Yeah, but now we can never go back."

Derp suddenly came to life as he slapped Kenny on the back of his skull. "What in the hell would ever make you want to go back? Scary goblin clowns tried to kill us to summon their ginormous clown god of destruction. Dude! No one in their right mind should want to go back to that."

"Derp has a point," I said. "I'd forget about the whole damned lot—magic, monsters, fae, everything—and walk away right now, if I could."

Derp raised a hand as if he needed my permission to speak. Kenny sighed in exasperation. "Derp, how many times do I have to tell you? You don't have to raise your hand every time you want to say something to an adult."

Derp dumped his last few fry crumbs into his mouth, then stared at the bottom of the paper bag with a sigh. "Yeah, but I never know the right time to interject my thoughts. It's easier when I raise my hand, because I don't end up talking all over everybody else. Adults hate it when you do that." I pushed my tray toward him, and he began munching on my fries as he continued. "Colin, I was just wondering... can't you get someone with psychic powers to mind-wipe you? You know, like Professor X or Jean Grey. Then you *could* walk away, right?"

I started to wonder if Derp had ESP, considering I'd just been thinking about mind-wiping *him*. "It doesn't work that way, unfortunately. Oh, I could get someone who knows mind magic to wipe my memory—but I've spent years dealing with the supernatural world. Having all those memories erased would likely destroy my mind and make me a vegetable.

"And even if I could have my memories erased without damaging my psyche, it still wouldn't keep the supernatural world from coming after me. I've made a lot of enemies over the years, and I'm sure there are many more that I don't even know about. Getting mind-wiped would just leave me vulnerable to them."

During this exchange, Kenny silently twisted a straw and watched it unwind itself, over and over again. He tossed the straw on the table and glared at me.

"You're going to have someone do that to us, aren't you?" he asked.

I tongued a molar and tsked. "Figured that out, did you?"

Derp looked back and forth at us. "Do what?" Realization dawned across his face, and he backed into his seat, waving both hands in front of him. "Aw, hell no! I don't want no mind flayer messing around inside my head. No way, no how. Uh-uh."

Kenny crossed his arms, never taking his eyes off me. "It's not fair. I'm the one who went in after Derp. If it wasn't for me, you'd never have rescued him. I have just as much right to know about them as you do."

"It's for your own good," I countered lamely.

Kenny threw his hands up in the air. "You just told us that if you got your memories erased, you'd be a sitting duck for them. Are you telling us those goblins aren't coming after us? That we'll be safe—that ignorance is bliss?"

Derp stole one of Kenny's leftover fries. "Dude, you have to stop quoting *The Matrix*. That movie is old—no one knows those quotes anymore."

I sat back in the booth, turning sideways and cocking a knee on the bench. "You sure you want to take the red pill? That's a big decision for a kid your age—one that can affect you and everybody you love for the rest of your life. Consider it carefully before you decide to jump feet-first into the unknown."

Kenny looked at Derp, and the unspoken question hung in the air between them. Derp ignored him, futzing with a pile of salt he'd poured onto the table. "Alright already, sheesh. No, Kenny, I don't want to go back to the way it was before. I mean, shit—how many people get to find out that their RPG fantasies are real?"

"And nightmares," I interjected. "Remember, you both came close to death tonight."

Derp nodded, still staring at the pile of salt he was pushing around. "Yeah, and that." He looked up, addressing us both. "But how could I ever go back to being the dork who gets de-pantsed in gym class every week, after surviving all that?"

That struck a chord with me, despite my reservations. Learning how to fight supernatural creatures had changed me, and Finnegas' presence and influence in my life had been nothing short of transformative. As much as I resented the old man for getting Jesse and me involved in the world of the fae, I had to admit that being a bullied high school nobody had sucked balls.

I looked hard at the boys. They returned my stare, Kenny with defiance in his eyes and Derp with hopeful expectation. I rubbed my forehead with both hands and exhaled slowly.

"I can't believe I'm saying this, but okay."

"Okay what?" Kenny asked.

"I'll let you two retain your memories... but only on a trial basis." They began to protest, and I cut them off. "Wait a minute, hear me out. I'll agree that I won't send some fae sorceress to wipe your minds in the middle of the night, if you two agree that you won't pursue the world beneath in any way, shape, or form for the next six months. Nor will you speak a word of it to anyone else! If you can stay out of trouble and keep quiet during that time, then I'll consider showing you how to defend yourselves from the supernatural."

Their faces broke into huge grins as they high-fived.

"Yes!" Kenny shouted.

"Do I get a magic sword?" Derp asked. "If so, I want a +5 vorpal blade!"

I covered my head with my hands and groaned. "What have I gotten myself into?"

SERPENT'S DAUGHTER

Note to readers: This narrative takes place after *Underground Druid*, so be warned—spoilers follow. If you haven't read Book 4 in the Colin McCool series yet, you might want to read it before you dive into this story.

12

I fell into step next to the dark wizard, latching onto his arm as I gently prodded him to increase his pace. Surprise registered on his lean, scarred face, which was only partially concealed inside the charcoal hoodie he wore beneath a mid-length black leather overcoat.

"You never fail to amaze, Belladonna. I thought I'd kept this trip under wraps."

"Keep walking, act normal, but pick it up a bit. We're being watched," I whispered as we headed out of the terminals at Santiago de Compostela Airport.

While the airport itself was a modern, high-ceilinged metal and glass structure, it was small, consisting of only one terminal with six gates. Galicia was a sizable Spanish province, and Santiago de Compostela was its regional capital. But we were still a backwater tourist destination, no matter how the city and region's leaders tried to show otherwise. That meant we'd have few opportunities to shake our tail. I'd have to time this properly, else we'd end up creating a scene and be detained by airport security—which was what the *mouros* wanted.

And that simply would not do. The Anjana did not take

failure lightly. She was a powerful fae witch who had bound my family to her service centuries ago, and she was every bit as ruthless and unforgiving as Queen Maeve back in Austin. She didn't like it when we attracted attention from the authorities, so the less trouble we caused shaking this tail, the better.

"I'm happy to see you're okay. You had us worried. But how did you know I was coming?" Crowley asked.

"Oh, I have my ways," I replied, trying to avoid staring at the scars the burns had left on his face and hand. I hadn't seen him since it had happened, and in a way, I'd been complicit in causing the chain of events that had led to his... *accident*? Yes, I suppose that was as good a description as any for what had occurred.

The wizard had once been my partner at the Cold Iron Circle—and, briefly, my lover. Crowley and I hadn't parted on the best of terms, so to have him here next to me now was a bit uncomfortable. The fact that he had once tried to kill my current boyfriend made the situation even more prickly.

"Since when have you cared to delve into the arts arcane?" he asked, as a sly smile crept across his ruined face. Hell and damnation, but he'd been beautiful once.

But now? Children pointed and stared, and parents pulled them away from the deformed man in the hood. The wizard, to his credit, did his best to ignore them. But I could see the tightness around his eyes as he pulled his hood down to better cover his face.

"I'll explain it all to you, but later. Right now, we need to shake our tail." We were coming up to the service entrance I'd prepared earlier as a secondary escape route. One of our contacts in the city had a cousin who worked at the airport, and they'd arranged to get me a keycard with limited access to the baggage processing areas. It would have to do.

"Get ready to move... now!" I pulled gently on Crowley's arm, signaling him to make a sharp turn around a corner and into an alcove, where I used the keycard to access a stairwell. "Alright, time to run. Did you bring any luggage with you?"

He held up a modest leather overnight bag as we bolted down the stairs. "Just my carry-on. I prefer to travel light, unlike some other people we know."

I had no doubt he was talking about my sometimes partner in crime and current love of my life, the druid Colin McCool. He habitually carried around a magical man purse that he called his "Craneskin Bag." The relic allowed him to store items in another dimension—anything small enough to fit in the opening of the bag. It was ugly as sin, but it had saved our hides more than once.

"If I had a bag of holding, you know I'd bring my entire wardrobe with me everywhere I went. A girl could get used to that."

We hit the bottom landing in lockstep, and I flashed the keycard at the reader on the wall next to the entrance to baggage processing. The LED turned green, and I yanked the door open.

Unfortunately, they were waiting for us.

"Damn it. Looks like we're in for a fight," I said as I pulled Crowley through the door and behind a luggage cart. The *duende* had taken out the airport employees who normally worked down here, disguising themselves in order to take their places. The illusions they hid behind would fool a normal mortal, but for someone like myself or Crowley, they stood out like Ted Nugent at a PETA protest.

Duende were somewhat akin to the red caps and bogles we dealt with back in Austin, the Spanish version of fae dwarves. However, they were much more adept at casting magic than your typical run-of-the-mill fae—especially illusions. They were fond of making you think they were in one place while they attacked from another direction, stabbing their prey in the back or hamstringing them. Despite their small size, they were not to be taken lightly.

Crowley quickly peeked over the baggage cart and ducked back down again.

"Did they see us?" I asked.

"Unfortunately, yes. They appear to have ended all pretense of being normal airport employees, and are now pulling out various bladed weapons."

"Can you take care of the cameras?"

"I can, and will." The wizard interlaced his fingers, and when he pulled them apart, a dark shadowy substance was strung between them like a cat's cradle. He worked it with his hands, then tossed it in the air. The shadow magic split in three, taking the form of inky little bats that flew toward every security camera in the room. Each of the flying shadow golems attached themselves firmly over the lenses, obscuring the view of any security personnel who might have been monitoring the area.

I reached under my coat and pulled out the pieces of the carbon-fiber crossbow pistol I'd snuck past the metal detectors. It wasn't ideal, but it was the best I could do under the circumstances. I assembled the weapon with a practiced alacrity, armed for battle seconds later.

"Well, if it's a fight they want..."

"... then I'd say it's best we oblige them," Crowley interjected. *Finishing my sentences. Just like old times.*

"I hate it when you do that," I said, just before I let the first crossbow bolt fly.

13

The carbon-fiber crossbow shafts were tipped with barbed holly points that I'd carved myself. Holly, like rowan wood, had particularly nasty effects on some fae. For the duende, they'd cause the expected physical damage and also disrupt their ability to cast spells—at least until they dug out the holly barbs.

I planted the first shaft in the groin of a tall lanky man with a bowl haircut and acne scars. He staggered, and his image shimmered and shifted until I was looking at a thin, four-foot-tall dwarf with a crossbow bolt sticking out of his chest.

Physically speaking, his appearance typified the unseelie fae among his kind. The duende had a pot belly, huge bare feet, heavily-muscled arms, and thick, callused hands. Dark beady eyes, a bulbous nose, and tight-set lips sat above a black Dutch beard, and a bright red *barretina* hat was perched atop his head. He held a rapier in his right hand and a parrying dagger in the other, which he stuck point-first into a nearby suitcase before pulling out the crossbow shaft.

Of course, the tip remained firmly embedded in his chest.

The dwarf looked at the bolt and scowled before he tossed it away, then he grabbed his dagger and charged me while I reloaded.

What I wouldn't give right now for a pair of Desert Eagles in .44 magnum, I thought.

I gave up on cocking the crossbow, and instead used it to parry a thrust from the dwarf's rapier, redirecting it to the inside as I kicked the little fae's lead knee. That threw him off balance, which momentarily prevented him from stabbing me with his dagger. I side-stepped past him and stabbed his right eye with a crossbow bolt, angling it down and in toward the brain stem.

The dwarf dropped like a rock. I snagged the rapier and dagger from his hands as he fell, flourishing them to check the balance and weight. *Ah, nothing like good Toledo steel.*

My little scuffle with the first dwarf had only lasted a few seconds, but that was enough time for two more of them to close in on me. Crowley was already at work, bouncing duende off the walls and floor with those creepy shadow tentacles of his. I only had a moment to glance his way before I was ducking a swing from a duende with a falcata.

The thugs the Ojáncanu had employed weren't playing around, that was for sure. Colin and Crowley's recent foray into the fae realm, and the subsequent fallout from their actions, had upset a balance of power that had lasted for centuries in the region. The old cyclops knew that the Anjana was vying for his magic, in a bid to keep him and his mouros living far underground where they belonged—and he was desperate to stop her. My job as one of the Anjana's flunkies was to make sure she succeeded. Crowley's magic could play a big part in that, which was why the Ojáncanu wanted him dead.

Did I feel bad that my old partner had walked blind into a centuries-old war between two powerful fae? A little, but I hadn't asked him to fly to Spain to check up on me. I could take care of myself, and I didn't need the men in my life to come to my rescue, thank you very much.

I was trapped between two of the duende, and the one with the falcata was trying to distract me so his companion could stick a dagger in my back. *Yeah, good luck with that.* I wasn't as naturally talented at swordplay as Colin, but Mother had taught me how to defend myself with all kinds of weapons, long before I'd ever gone to work for the Circle.

The only problem was, I couldn't effectively fight two of them at once—at least not with one at my back. I needed to take one of them out quickly. I faked a thrust at the swordsman's eyes then switched direction, charging the one with the knives. It was my best bet, since the rapier had more reach than those daggers. I thrust at the duende's knee, wounding him, then I beat his half-hearted stabbing attack away and skewered him through the neck.

Unfortunately, the rapier got lodged in his spine. Now, I'd have to face down falcata-boy with a parrying dagger. *Great.*

I dove over the one I'd just killed, grabbing one of his daggers from the floor as I rolled back to my feet to face the swordsman. The thing about a falcata was that it was a chopping weapon, and not the best implement for stabbing and thrusting. If I could get this duende to commit to an attack, I might get inside the reach of his blade and end him.

I retreated a half-step as the dwarf walked over his dead companion. As I did, I faked a stumble, letting my heel hit the edge of a piece of luggage that had been knocked off the conveyor in the struggle. That was all it took to get the little guy to charge me, his sword held in a high guard.

I threw one of the daggers at his face in an awkward under-hand toss. It wasn't meant to do any damage, only to distract him. As I expected, he moved the pommel and guard of the sword to deflect the knife, obscuring his vision for a split second. That was all the opening I needed. I grabbed his wrist with my free hand as I closed the gap, and drove the blade in my other hand under his chin and up into his brain.

14

I spun in a half-circle with the dwarf's falcata in hand, looking for more attackers.

The remaining duende were bloody, twisted lumps scattered here and there in the baggage processing area. Apparently, Crowley had been busy while I'd been preoccupied. The wizard leaned against a metal support column as he clapped slowly.

"Didn't care to lend a hand with those two?" I asked.

"And spoil your fun? Please. I remember well how you hated being 'rescued' back when we were partners. I doubt that a few weeks of dating a mildly-chauvinist druid would have changed that."

"You doubted right." I retrieved my crossbow bolts and wiped my fingerprints off the weapons I'd touched. "We need to leave—other duende will be along shortly."

Crowley gestured at the bodies. "Shouldn't we clean this up?"

I shook my head. "Don't worry about it. Duende are self-cleaning." As I spoke, the corpses began crumbling. Within moments, nothing remained but small piles of fine brown dust.

"Well, that's convenient," Crowley remarked.

"Their boss has them spelled, so if someone kills one of them they won't have proof of the duende's existence."

"And if they're captured?"

I shrugged. "They commit suicide. Let's go."

I started walking toward a service hall, opposite the door we'd entered through, and Crowley fell in step beside me. We exited the building through a side entrance that led to the tarmac, then snuck around the side. I'd cut a hole in the fence earlier, and we slipped through the gap. From there, it was a short walk to the parking lot.

"Do you care to tell me what's going on?" he asked.

I ignored him as I headed toward a jet-black Porsche Cayenne Turbo with dark limo tint and custom wheels. "Our ride. Hop in, and I'll explain everything."

Crowley whistled. "Hunting must pay well in Spain." The approval in his voice reminded me that he liked expensive things... or at least he had, once.

I hit the ignition and the twin-turbo V8 thrummed with the velvet growl of 550 finely-tuned horses. I shifted into gear and took us out of the airport parking lot and onto the highway, heading to the southwest for the mountains of the Serra do Candán, my ancestral home. Once we were on the highway and well away from the airport, I spoke.

"What do you know about Spanish folklore?" I asked.

"Not much, except that the mythology is similar to that of Ireland and Scotland, mostly due to the shared Celtic origins. As evidenced by the fae we just killed. I'd say those—what did you call them?"

"Duende."

"Right. I'd say they're close relatives of the red caps, kissing cousins at least. So, why were they waiting for me at the airport, how did you know I was coming, and why do these duende want to kill us?"

"Long story short? Centuries ago, my family made a pact with a fae witch, pledging our eternal loyalty in exchange for magic and wealth. Our job was to help her keep her father and his underlings from encroaching on human lands, which we'd done successfully with the help of her magic. Until now."

The women of my family had been magically bound to the Anjana for years, becoming *mouras encantadas*, guardians of the gates to the Underrealms. I'd bucked tradition by going to America to work for the Cold Iron Circle—under the pretense of attending college there, of course.

Truth was, the Anjana creeped me out, and I didn't much like the idea of embracing that part of my heritage. In my opinion, we were just pawns in a centuries-old struggle between the Anjana and her father, the Ojáncanu. He was the king of the mouros, and a mortal enemy of our mistress. She lacked the foot soldiers that the Ojáncanu had at his command, so she'd enlisted my family as her servants. She'd promised them gold and riches in exchange for their eternal loyalty, as well as magic to fight the Ojáncanu's duende, who had been a thorn in my family's side for years.

The Anjana had delivered on her promise, and my family had become powerful and wealthy beyond belief. But that wealth and power came at a steep price—one I didn't personally care to pay. And once I officially pledged my loyalty and accepted her magic, I'd be hers, forever. That was why I'd initially failed to answer my mother's summons. I simply did not care to be at the Anjana's beck and call for the rest of my life.

Unfortunately, the situation had recently changed. When Colin had closed the pathways to Underhill, it had weakened the Anjana considerably. And while much of her magic was anchored in nature, having her connection to the Underrealms severed meant she was vulnerable to attack. That's why I'd come home, to aid Mother and the Anjana in any way I could. It was my duty, after all... no matter how much I wanted to deny it.

At some point, I intended to settle matters between Mother, the Anjana, and me for good—to establish that I wasn't going to be in the Anjana's service forever. I just needed to find the right leverage to negotiate my freedom. I had high hopes that Crowley could help me with that.

Crowley pulled a handkerchief from inside his coat and wiped his injured eye, which still remained concealed within his hood. "It appears that our recent trip to Underhill has had repercussions that reach further than even I would have guessed."

My voice dripped with sarcasm, and I barely held my temper in check as I responded. "You think? Now that the pathways to the Underrealms are cut off, the Anjana's power is considerably weaker. Her father, the Ojáncanu, knows we're weak. He's sent several probing attacks over the last several weeks. If he comes out of hiding, it'll be a disaster. He's a traditional giant, Crowley, with a traditional diet."

"I take it he's not a vegetarian."

I snorted. "Hardly. When he and his kind lived topside, they terrorized my ancestors. The mouros, our version of the fae, weren't exactly the friendly kind. The Ojáncanu imprisoned his own daughter for centuries, forcing her to guard the entrance to the caverns where he lived. Can you imagine enslaving your own daughter? It boggles the mind."

Crowley remained silent for a few moments. Something I said must've hit a nerve. "And this Anjana—that's the witch you spoke of?"

"The same. My ancestors helped free her from the spell her father had cast to imprison her. Unbound, she's incredibly powerful—more so than her father, in fact. At least, she was, until Colin screwed things up. Now, she's vulnerable. We all are."

"We—meaning you and your family, I presume?"

"Yup. Mom, my cousins, and I."

Crowley slowly drummed his fingers on his knee. "For the record, I had no idea of his plans. No one did, I think, save the Tuatha Dé Danann with whom he held council."

"I don't even want to know, because the more I know the more it's going to piss me off. What was he thinking? I mean, what gave him the right to commit an act that would have such far-reaching consequences? When I see him..." I slammed my hand on the steering wheel and growled.

"Far be it from me to defend Colin's actions, or to intercede in a lover's dispute. However, I'm sure he had very good reasons for doing what he did. And despite the ordeal he suffered because of it, you were the first person he asked for when Finnegas finally located him."

I chewed my lip and thought about what I was going to do to that boy when I saw him. I teetered back and forth between kicking his ass and jumping his bones. I'd probably settle for angry sex when the moment came. I was seriously pissed at him, but damn it if I didn't miss him.

"Is he okay? You don't know how many times I nearly left Mom and the rest to search for him."

"I just saw him before I left. In fact, he's the reason why I'm here. Why didn't you send word to him, before you left?"

"Like he sent word to me before you all went traipsing off into Underhill? Hah! I wanted to make him sweat a little." Crowley sniffed, which was the equivalent of a gasp coming from him. "Oh, please. I had people keeping tabs on the situation, believe me. I knew the moment he got back from wherever Finnegas found him. But after that stunt he pulled, he deserved to stew a little."

"He left you behind for a reason, Belladonna. Travelling to Underhill can have deleterious effects on mortals. Although I get the feeling that you're not exactly mortal, are you?"

I held a hand out and wavered it back and forth. "Meh, sort of. I don't get my powers until I officially join the cult. That's why Mom wanted me back home, and it's also why I left in the first place. I'm not exactly down with serving the Anjana for the next couple of centuries, and I kind of resent that some bitch way back in my family tree took it upon herself to make that decision for me."

"Understandable. I take it your mother doesn't approve of your rebellion?"

I snickered. "Hardly. But enough with my mommy issues. The question is, what am I going to do with you?"

Crowley chuckled. "I could think of a few things, although I don't think Colin would approve."

"Flirting, Crowley? Really? After the way we split?"

He held his hands up defensively. "I'm just glad you're speaking with me. Suffice it to say that I regret my past indiscretions. Truce?"

"For now. But Mom might have other ideas. You're not exactly high on her list of favorite people."

15

My family occupied a small, secluded mountain village, far away from prying eyes. The roads that led to our home were under a powerful "look away, go away" spell, and that was sufficient to keep everyone out who didn't belong. Well, that, and the rumors that had been spread over the centuries about the evil, blood-drinking witches who occupied the mountain.

As we pulled into the walled villa I'd grown up in, I gauged Crowley's reaction. I wouldn't have necessarily called our home opulent, but it was apparent that we had money. I'd never really felt self-conscious about it. At least, not until Mother had sent me away to attend private school in the U.S. There, everyone's social status was directly related to their wealth—a fact which I found repulsive.

After I'd shoved a girl's head in the toilet for telling me to go back to Mexico—the idiot couldn't tell a European Spanish accent from a North American one—the other students mostly left me alone. However, that experience had taught me that wealth of the type I had enjoyed growing up was the province of a very small minority. I also saw how wealth divided people, how it made people treat you differently.

People assumed things about the wealthy, just as they did about the poor, and that was why I chose to live rather frugally back in Austin. I wondered whether Colin would look at me any differently if he ever saw how I'd grown up. He never would, if I could help it, because it simply wasn't worth the risk.

"Not a word about any of this to Colin when you get home," I said.

"My lips are sealed. Nice mansion, by the way."

"If you mention anything about this to him..."

"Relax, I won't speak of it. However, if you're as serious about him as I think you are, don't you think he's going to find out about it eventually?"

"I'll cross that bridge when I'm damned good and ready." When I pulled into the circular drive, Mom was waiting for us at the front entrance. She wasn't clairvoyant; she had GPS tracking devices installed on all the vehicles for security reasons. I put the car in park, pausing before I stepped out of the vehicle.

"Don't say I didn't warn you about Mother," I said.

"Noted," the dark wizard replied.

I got out and approached my mother, who stared down at me imperiously. She was a tall, beautiful woman—thin, elegant, and intimidating. I'd inherited my father's height, unfortunately, and failed to take after her in that regard. Why mother had married such a short man was beyond me, but such was love. I stopped in front of her and clasped my hands behind my back, awaiting questions.

She spoke to me in Spanish, although I doubted that she thought it would provide any privacy around Crowley. She merely did it to be rude. "Did you have any problems from the duende?"

I chose to answer in English. Mother hated when I did that. "A minor scuffle. No one saw, Crowley made certain of that."

As Crowley joined us, Mother glanced over at him and scowled. "This is the wizard who broke your heart and sullied your reputation?"

"Yes, Mama."

"And you let him live?"

"I couldn't exactly murder him over a verbal indiscretion, Mama. My employer frowns on such things."

"This Cold Iron Circle, they sound much too modern to do the work we do effectively. The mouros do not obey the rules of man. How can we keep them at bay if we choose to do so?" She tsked. "I will never understand why you decided to work for them, instead of taking your rightful place with us."

"Not now, Mother. We have a guest."

She spared him a sideways sneer. "Have it your way, *mi hija.* But I will have words with this one." She turned to Crowley and addressed him in English. "You insulted my daughter. You hurt her. This, I cannot forgive."

He pulled his hood back to look her in the eye, revealing his ruined face. "I agree. My actions were reprehensible. I can assure you, I'm a changed man since then—and I would make amends, if possible."

She smiled like the serpent in the garden. "You'll have ample opportunity to do so while you're here, but can you?"

Crowley arched an eyebrow. "Can I..."

"Can you be of use to us, wizard? You do owe my daughter a debt of honor, but can you repay it? You're mortal, that much is plain—yet there's something about you, a darkness that clings to you, that is a part of you. This darkness, it is the source of your magic, yes?"

Crowley shrugged.

"A test, then. Yes, that would be best, before I take you to the

Anjana. No sense in burdening her with your presence if you're of no use to her."

She clapped her hands, and three of my cousins appeared. They'd been hiding behind columns, among the shrubbery, and the like. Mother gestured to the circular grassy area bordered by the driveway.

"Wizard, if you'll be so kind as to indulge me?"

Crowley looked at me, and I sighed. "I warned you," I said.

He pulled his hood back up and stepped into the center of the lawn. "I am at your disposal, Señora Becerra."

Mother called to my cousins, Alicia, Fabiana, and Luna. Each were carbon copies of the others with dark hair and eyes, light olive skin, and a dancer's muscles. They were all older than me, and fully vested in the powers the Anjana had granted to them. The girls were tall and graceful like Mother, and well-trained like me—but that wasn't what made them deadly. This would not be a fair fight.

Crowley already knew he was dealing with something supernatural, but the nature of their powers would be a mystery to him. Wisely, he spooled up his power, casting tendrils of shadow magic around him. They whipped and waved in the air in random patterns—a trick he used in combat to cause confusion when faced with multiple opponents.

The girls spread out, then they transformed and attacked.

16

A little secret about me and my family that I hadn't told anyone—we were shifters. Lamiae, to be exact. Well, all the women in my family were, except me. I chose not to accept the Anjana's "gift," which made me a bit of a black sheep among my relatives.

My cousins, however, were full-on snake people. When the girls shifted, it happened in an instant. One minute, Crowley was facing three beautiful, harmless-looking girls, and the next he was facing three were-serpents. Each girl was human from the waist up—naked, no less, as the shift happened magically and not physically—with a giant serpent's body from the waist down.

Their upper bodies changed as well, but not as drastically. The girls now displayed long upper and lower fangs; their tongues had lengthened and become forked; and their eyes were reptilian rather than human. And, their fingers ended in sharp claws. Fabiana and Luna's skin was mostly still human, with only the occasional scale showing here and there. But Alicia, the oldest of the three, was more mature in her control of her powers. Her upper body was covered in scales. The scales were protective in nature, and they made it harder to injure her.

Crowley, ever the pragmatist, shot a bolt of shadow magic at the nearest girl to him, Luna. It hit her in the face and stuck like spider-silk, covering her mouth and eyes and obscuring her vision. She screamed in a muffled, frustrated wail, and clawed at the dark mist covering her face, but her efforts had zero effect.

On seeing their companion go down, Fabiana and Alicia attacked simultaneously. A shadow arm shot out and grabbed Fabiana by the throat, wrapping around her neck to hold her several paces away. Crowley did to her what she had intended to do to him, and her face turned red, then purple as he choked her into unconsciousness.

But Alicia had dodged Crowley's attack, coming in low on her belly in a slithering sprint. She closed the gap and dove at his leg, obviously intending to sink her fangs into his thigh. She wouldn't inject enough poison to kill him, but only enough to end the fight. Fortunately, Crowley was way too slick for her. Instead of getting a mouthful of flesh, she sunk her fangs into a layer of shadow that had been hovering, almost invisibly, just above his skin.

Fabiana and Luna were on the ground by this time, and Crowley released his magic from them both. In similar fashion, Crowley's shadow mist crawled its way into Alicia's mouth and down her throat, where I assumed it was meant to fill her lungs and prevent her from breathing. But she wasn't going down without a fight. Her tail whipped around and swept Crowley's legs out from under him, forcing him to use his shadow tentacles to support his weight.

That's what Alicia wanted. She was crafty, that girl, and calm under pressure. Even as she fought for breath, she was planning how to eke out victory. With his shadow limbs preoccupied,

Alicia was able to whip her tail around and wrap it around the wizard's torso. Then, she squeezed.

Crowley's magic wavered and weakened, and every tendril of magic but the one attached to Alicia's mouth disappeared. As my cousin did her best to crush the life out of the wizard, he remained focused on maintaining that single shred of his magic to smother her. What it boiled down to now was a battle of wills.

I checked my watch. Fifteen seconds passed, then thirty seconds, then forty-five. Alicia was squeezing Crowley hard enough to crush his ribs, and I was certain she would have, if he hadn't been intervening with his magic. His hood had fallen away from his face, and his mouth worked like a fish out of water, desperately attempting to force air into his lungs. Still, he persisted.

Likewise, Alicia's jaws were stretched wide by Crowley's magic, and her eyes bulged from her head. Her face was distorted and discolored, and tears ran from her eyes. They would kill each other before either gave up the fight.

"Mama, enough..." I began to say, but she silenced me with a single raised finger.

Mother never took her eyes off them, intent on seeing who would be the victor. Finally, after ninety seconds had passed, she snapped her fingers. "Alicia, enough."

Alicia continued to squeeze.

"I said enough!" Mother's voice rumbled with authority. She was not one to be trifled with, and my cousin knew it. Her eyes shot back and forth between Crowley and Mother, then she relented, releasing the wizard. He withdrew his magic, and the two fell gasping on the ground next to one another.

Mother turned to me. "When he's recovered, you're to take him to the Anjana immediately. She's already informed me that he'll be instrumental in helping us wrest control of the *Piscina de Cristal* from the mouros."

Mother strode off into the house, leaving me to handle the fallout from the short battle that had taken place. Fabiana and Luna had recovered and switched back to their human shapes, while Alicia had chosen to remain in her were-serpent form. She pushed herself off the ground, coiling to attack Crowley again. He was still gasping on the ground, and in no shape to defend himself.

I pulled a .44 magnum revolver from beneath my jacket and cocked the hammer as I pointed it at her. "Don't even think about it, Alicia."

She turned her serpent's eyes on me and smiled. "Relax, *prima*. I was only going to give him a little love bite—something to remember me by."

"Back away, Alicia. Mother says the Anjana needs him."

Alicia turned back toward Crowley. "Then she can heal him."

I fired the pistol at the ground next to her coiled snake body. "The next one goes in your gut. Then you'll be the one asking the Anjana to heal you."

She swiveled to face me again and narrowed her eyes. "Fine. But point a gun at me again, and I'll make you eat it."

I kept the gun on her, watching her like a hawk until she transformed back into her human form and walked away with Fabiana and Luna tagging along behind her.

After they were gone, I holstered the pistol and helped Crowley sit up.

"Is that how your mother always greets guests?" he croaked.

"Only the ones who break her daughter's heart."

He felt his ribs and winced. "I swear on my scars, I'll never do that again."

17

C rowley stood statue still as I wrapped his bruised ribs. He'd initially told me he didn't need first aid, until I'd pointed out that the bandages would support his ribs until his magic healed him. Finally, he reluctantly agreed, the silly male that he was. Men and their egos...

He took a selfie of me bandaging him, for what reason I had no idea. I had to admit, I was impressed that he didn't flinch once, because he'd used to be a big baby. I guess getting half his face burned off had taught him something about dealing with pain.

"What's this 'crystal pool' your mother spoke of?" he asked as I applied the last piece of kinesio tape to his ribs.

"The Piscina de Cristal is the source of the mouros' power now. It's a power sink that gathers and stores magic from nature. Whether they stumbled across it ages ago, or if they created it themselves, no one can say—not even the Anjana. Since she's cut off from Underhill right now, her magical reserves are low."

As he pulled his shirt down, I admired his abs on the sly. One thing was for certain, his body wasn't scarred... not in the slightest.

"I take it the Anjana sees the pool as a vital resource that will assure her continued existence?"

"And ours. The Ojáncanu and his forces could storm right out of the caverns and steamroll us if they wanted. Granted, my mother and the rest of the women in my family are powerful shifters, but we're outnumbered. Without the Anjana's magic backing us up, we'll be toast."

The dark wizard hopped off the table. "Thus, the reason why the Anjana thinks I'll be useful in gaining control of this magical well. You need a magic wielder to even the odds."

"Exactly. And, since you conveniently decided to come looking for me, you got volunteered for the mission... the details of which we'll get from the Anjana."

Crowley seemed to consider this for a moment, although it was difficult to tell what his face was doing inside that cowl. But I had been his working partner at the Circle for months, and his lover for a short time. I knew from his body language what he was thinking.

"You're suspicious," I said.

"Of many things... but in particular, of your family situation, your strained relationship with your mother, of how that impacts your relationship to this Anjana you speak of, and whether she is manipulating you to her own ends."

Leave it to a man to state the obvious and make it seem like keen insight. "She's fae, Crowley—so of course she's manipulating me. Spanish fae, but fae just the same. And as for your next question —what she wants from me? I think you can guess based on what you've seen today."

"Hmmm. I take it that you want to refuse the Anjana's 'gift' of serpenthropy. And she wants to trick you into accepting it, thus binding you to her service." He paused, tapping a finger on his chin. "Belladonna, why have I not seen any men around here, in your family's compound?"

"I was wondering when you'd get around to asking about that. That's one of the reasons I don't want to commit myself to the Anjana's cause. My family is fiercely matriarchal—so much so that we never marry, and we don't enter into long-term relationships with men."

"With men, you say?" he remarked, with unveiled amusement in his voice.

"You just couldn't leave that one alone, could you, Crowley? Wipe those fantasies from your mind, pig, because I'm not gay. However, several of the women in my family are, just so you know. Anyway, we live like Amazons. We mate to breed, and that's about it."

"Uh-huh. So, I was just supposed to be a fling?"

"I'm not having that discussion with you right now." Mostly because I'd only dated Crowley to make Colin jealous. It had still hurt when he'd betrayed me, but that was water under the bridge. "Set your man-brain aside, and let's stay on task. The Anjana is going to ask us to do the impossible, which is par for the course with the fae. She needs your help to complete this mission, which means she needs me to guide you. That should provide us with some leverage when we negotiate with her."

"Ah, you intend to cut a deal for your freedom."

I pursed my lips and nodded. "Yep. She's more vulnerable now than ever, and I may not have a chance to bargain with her again. This is my opportunity to be rid of any obligations to her that I inherited, once and for all."

"I suppose I can see how you'd want to be free from"—he gestured expansively—"all of this."

"Are you being sarcastic?"

"Not at all," he said as he wagged a finger at me. Crowley could be so condescending. "Please don't take this the wrong way, Belladonna, but you're simply not cut out for a life of celibacy and service. You're way too headstrong. And... amorous, if that's the right word."

I exhaled heavily and rolled my eyes. He was really asking for a punch to the throat. "You do realize you're walking on thin ice right now?"

"I do, but before I embark on yet another impossible quest for the fae on behalf of a friend, I'd simply like to be crystal-clear as to your motives."

"My motives are simple. Number one, make sure that my family isn't forced from their ancestral home by the Ojáncanu and his mouros. And second, I hope to make the Anjana so indebted to me that she agrees to let me do as I please."

"A question... why don't you just go back to the States? Surely her reach doesn't extend halfway around the world."

I carefully considered how to answer him, and decided that if he was voluntarily getting mixed up in my troubles, he deserved the truth. "Part of it has to do with family and obligation," I said. "But mostly I'm doing this out of self-preservation."

"Come again?"

"Crowley, throughout the years, any member of my family who reneged on their obligation to the Anjana was hunted down by the rest of the clan and killed."

"Without exception?"

I nodded. "So, are you in, or out?"

"When you put it that way... when do we leave?"

18

A well-worn path led from our villa up into the foothills. Crowley and I walked the trail, along with an escort that consisted of Fabiana and another of my cousins, Julieta. Julieta had still been a kid when I'd left, a fourteen-year-old beanpole with a wicked spin kick and a gap between her top front teeth. At seventeen and fresh out of braces, she was a raven-haired knockout—in more ways than one.

Mother had insisted on the escort. After the incident at the airport, she feared that the duende and mouros were getting bolder, and that they might even attempt to attack us openly in our territory. Thankfully, Alicia wanted nothing to do with us, so she'd stayed back at the villa with the rest of the clan. As we ascended the path to the Anjana's home, the girls peppered Crowley with questions.

"What's it like, living in America?" Fabiana asked. Apparently, her defeat at Crowley's hands hadn't injured her pride at all. To my cousin, it merely meant he was good breeding material. "Are all Americans as fat and stupid as they say?"

Crowley's head swiveled as he scanned the surrounding pine and eucalyptus trees. "Not all of them, no."

The wizard's answers had been curt and polite, but not encouraging of their interest in him. *How curious.* Crowley had once considered himself to be quite the ladies' man. Either he had changed, or he had other interests.

Julieta snickered. "I read that two-thirds of Americans are overweight. That must make them easy prey for the fae and other supernatural predators. Not like us, eh, Fabiana?" She did a sort of one-handed cartwheel into an *au batido*, a banana kick from capoeira. *Showing off for Crowley, little cousin?*

Fabiana glanced over her shoulder at me. "The fatness appears to be catching. Our prima looks to have gotten fatter during her stay in America."

Bitch! My cousins were all tall and willowy, while I was built more like a gymnast—short, with powerful hips and thighs. Colin certainly hadn't complained about my Shakira booty, but during my childhood I'd been teased by my cousins for being short and "fat."

I kept my voice calm and steady as I replied. "I've put on some muscle since you last saw me, Fabiana. And I can still kick your ass."

Fabiana snorted. "Not without the *magia de serpientropía.* I too have become stronger in your absence, cousin."

"But not smarter, apparently. Need I remind you that I deal with 'thropes all the time in my work? Believe me, I don't need magic to deal with the likes of you."

Fabiana gave me a dirty look. Julieta waited until she wasn't looking, then smirked at me and rolled her eyes at Fabiana's back. The kid was alright. Fabiana chose to remain silent for the remainder of the hike to the Anjana's glade. I chatted amiably with Julieta until we arrived at the entrance, then the pair left us and took up posts to await our return. No one entered the Anjana's presence unless summoned.

I led Crowley farther up the path to our private meeting with the ancient fae witch, and we soon entered the small clearing that surrounded the Anjana's serene, spring-fed pond. The sorceress herself sat on a boulder along the shore, leaning over the water and gazing into its depths. I motioned for Crowley to remain silent, then waited patiently for her to recognize our presence.

The Anjana was as she'd always been, for as long as I'd known her. Full-figured and voluptuous in a manner that was long out of vogue, she could have been a twin to Botticelli's Venus. Hell, for all I knew, she *was* Botticelli's Venus. Her long red hair fell in wavy cascades down her shoulders and back, starkly contrasting her creamy, pale skin and setting off her rosy cheeks and full, cherry-stained lips.

Her bright, almost luminescent blue eyes regarded us as she waved me over.

"Belladonna, my stray lamb. I understand the duende caused you some trouble at the airport. I hope you and your companion escaped unharmed?"

I gave just the slightest nod. Composure and careful speech were the rule of the day around the Anjana. Despite how *anjanas* were portrayed in the folk tales of our country, *our* Anjana was far from benevolent. She was known to be cruel and vindictive, taking vengeance for even the smallest slight months or even years after events had occurred, when the person who raised her ire had long forgotten the incident.

"We did, Doña Anjana. They were of no consequence."

A coy smile played at the corner of her sensuous mouth. "I see that time has not diminished your confidence, *princesa*. Nor your brutal efficiency."

I inclined my head slightly. "You trained me well, Doña Anjana."

"As was my right. And yet, look how you've repaid my matronage. You lied to your mother—to us all, really—and rent your gifts and talents to those bumbling American late-comers. Is this fair, my lovely? Is it just?"

"With respect, Doña Anjana, I never chose this life."

The Anjana turned her attention back to the waters, trailing her hand along the surface and watching the droplets return to their source. "None choose their own fate, *princesa*. Neither the high-born nor low-born, neither queens nor peasants. Humans only think they chart their own course, but in truth they are tossed to and fro by circumstances they cannot foresee or control.

"You had the good fortune to be born into power and wealth, yet you would forsake it all. And for what? A boy? This does not become one of your lineage, Belladonna."

"I love him, Doña Anjana."

She hissed softly and her eyes flashed with anger. "'Love is a serious mental illness.' Do you know who said that? Plato."

"'Unable are the loved to die, for love is immortality.'"

Her demeanor changed in an instant as she laughed, her voice a bubbling brook that echoed across the glade. "I forget what it is to be young and foolish. You have always been full of surprises, *princesa*."

She turned her eyes back to me. Rather than lowering my own as I should have, I chose to meet her gaze.

"I know what you wish for, Belladonna. You want to be free from the pact your ancestors made with me. You want to pursue love. But I have seen your future, and that of the druid. It is not meant to be. This path will only bring you sorrow."

"With respect, Doña Anjana, it's a risk I'm willing to take."

She nodded once. "I cannot release you, but I am willing to give you time to see the error of your ways. Take the wizard to the *Terreno de los Mouros*, and return with the Piscina de Cristal. Do this for me, and I will grant you ten years to do as you will, to experience the pain love always brings.

"But listen, *princesa*, and listen well. At the end of those ten years, your life and service will be mine, to do with as I see fit. And if you refuse me then, I will turn you to stone and you will serve me forever by decorating my glade."

It wasn't what I'd hoped for, but it was something. The reprieve would give me time to figure out a way to escape the Anjana's clutches for good.

"I will do this thing for you, Doña Anjana. I swear it."

She waved me away with a slow sweep of her hand and resumed gazing at the clear, still waters. "Be gone, then, and do not return until you have the Piscina."

19

Rather than returning the way we'd come, Crowley and I headed out the other side of the Anjana's glade. Mother had assured me that the Anjana's magic would see us quickly to our destination, although the entrance to the Ojáncanu's cavern was miles away from the witch's demesne. We'd only walked a few hundred yards before the dense forests of the foothills thinned out, giving way to the rocky crags and peaks of the mountains above.

"Did you get what you wanted from her?" the wizard asked.

"In a manner of speaking, yes. She agreed to give me ten years to do as I please before she sends my family after me. That is, so long as we return with the Piscina."

"Speaking of which, I take it this thing is portable?"

I paused as I scanned our surroundings for familiar landmarks. From the time we were little, the women in my clan were brought up here on scouting and surveillance missions, to ensure that the mouros were not roaming above ground. Occasionally, those expeditions turned violent, when we'd run into duende or other creatures. Sometimes, girls didn't make it back.

"Yes. From what I understand, it's something like a bird bath —like a piece of decorative statuary."

"And how did you plan to carry this thing out after we find it?"

I cracked my neck and massaged the muscles at the base of my skull. All this tension was giving me a headache and putting me off my game. "Well, I thought that you could carry it—or, rather, one of your shadow golems."

"If so, that means you'll need to do most of the fighting," he said. "While my magic is... self-sustaining, I have a limited pool from which to draw. If I split off part of my power to create a golem, my abilities will be diminished."

I pulled back my jacket to reveal an Uzi submachine pistol on a shoulder sling, my Desert Eagles, and a tactical belt loaded with several spare magazines. "I expected as much. But after we sneak in and find it, we'll likely be running and gunning on the way out. If we're flanked, you'll need to drop the thing and engage the enemy. As good as I am, I can't effectively fight in two directions at once."

"Don't worry, I have your back." He approached me and spun his finger in circles. "Turn around."

I arched an eyebrow and did as he asked. Crowley began to use those long, slender fingers to knead the knots out of my neck and shoulders. At first, I wasn't at all comfortable with the physical contact—but it felt so good I relented momentarily. I'd forgotten just how pleasing Crowley's hands could be.

Moments later, guilt took over and I stepped away, rolling my shoulders and neck out. I turned to the wizard with a half-hearted frown.

"Does Colin know you're trying to steal me back?"

His hood bobbed up and down. "He said he expected it. He didn't seem to be worried about the competition. I think he takes you for granted, Belladonna."

No, that just means he trusts me. A smile played across my lips. Damn it, but I missed that stubborn, awkward man-boy. "C'mon, let's go. I think I know where we're at. The cavern entrance isn't far."

Crowley's body language told me we weren't finished with that conversation. He squared his shoulders and walked stiffly as he followed me up rocky switchback trails that were better suited to goats than humans. We rounded a large boulder and I pointed up to a shadowed cleft in the side of the mountain.

"There. That's where we're headed."

"It looks unguarded."

I chuckled. "I can assure you, it's not. There's a *cuegle* that lives just inside the mouth of the cavern. The Ojáncanu lets him live there in exchange for guarding the entrance to his demesne."

"A cuegle?"

I chewed my lip and pulled out a small spotting scope, using it to scan the entrance to the cave. "It's a sort of troll. Three arms, three eyes, ugly and strong as hell. Hard to hurt, harder to kill, and honey badger vicious. They eat humans, by the way."

"And just how do you propose we get past this creature?"

I put the spotting scope back in my jacket. The cuegle was definitely up there, because every once in a while he'd pop his head up to search the area for trespassers. He hadn't seen us yet, but there was no way to avoid being spotted as we approached the only entrance to the underground home of the mouros. I cursed myself for failing to bring a sniper rifle along.

"My plan was to take the direct route." I drew one of my pistols and checked to make sure I had a round in the chamber.

Crowley placed a hand on my arm. "Hang on a minute. Isn't the idea to sneak into this cave? If you go in guns blazing, it'll certainly alert them to our presence."

I shrugged. "We fight our way in, and fight our way back out again. I know it lacks elegance, but it's as good a plan as any."

The wizard rubbed his chin. "But, perhaps, not necessary. You say this creature is extremely aggressive?" I nodded. "We might use that to our advantage. Give me a few moments to come up with an alternative solution."

He sat cross-legged on a small boulder nearby, out of sight of the cuegle, and closed his eyes. As his breathing slowed he began working shadow magic in his hands, almost like he was pulling taffy. The magic stretched and grew the more he worked with it, and he shaped it into a roughly humanoid thing that was more or less the size of a small child. The surface of the golem glistened wetly, like used engine oil or hot tar, and its eyeless head swiveled left and right as it tested its limbs.

Crowley opened his eyes and examined his work. "It's the best I could do on short notice, but it should suffice."

"What is it?" I asked, with equal amounts of wonder and repulsion in my voice.

"Are you familiar with the tales of Anansi the Spider?" he asked.

20

The creepy shadow golem waddled its way up the trail toward the cavern entrance, like a precocious toddler testing the boundaries of its environment. I noted that, as it walked, its feet collected small pebbles and bits of dirt that adhered to its surface. Within seconds, the rocks were absorbed into the golem, increasing its mass slightly as it progressed.

"It's a tar doll," I stated, amused. "Think it'll work?"

"I assure you, once the cuegle attacks the doll, it will be stuck fast. At some point, the golem will dissipate and my magic will return—so it would behoove us to be near the cavern's entrance when the creature is immobilized. Hopefully, it will be so preoccupied with freeing itself we'll be able to sneak right past."

Thankfully, the sun was still on the other side of the mountains, leaving plenty of shade in which to hide. The wizard cloaked us in shadow, and we darted from boulder to boulder until we reached a concealment point a few yards from the cavern opening.

I peeked around the edge of the rock; the cuegle had its back turned to us. Opposite our position, the tar doll awkwardly leveraged itself up and over the ledge—in full view of the creature.

The cuegle was just as ugly as I remembered. I'd seen him, once, when I was just a child. We'd come up here on a scouting expedition, and the creature had ambushed the group I'd been accompanying. I'd watched as he'd torn one of my cousins in two.

The cuegle was roughly five-and-a-half feet tall—more or less my height, but with a much stockier build. He had charcoal-colored skin, three eyes and three arms, a single horn in his forehead above his third eye, and a mouthful of sharp, crooked teeth. There were bones strewn around the cave mouth—some human, some animal—and the stench of rotten flesh lingered in the thin mountain air.

As the golem levered itself over the cliff edge and stood, the cuegle's head swiveled toward it with a growl. The tar doll simply stood there, glistening and wobbling slightly—just the way a small human child might. Apparently, the cuegle found that movement irresistible, because he ran at the golem and pounced on it, pinning it to the ground with two of his three arms.

The result was instantaneous and hilarious. As the cuegle made contact with the doll, the golem sort of squished as it enveloped the creature's club-like hands. He tried to pull one hand away, but it was stuck fast. He yanked with the other arm, only succeeding in stretching the golem slightly before getting that limb stuck too.

Confused by these events, the cuegle roared and struck the golem's head with his third arm. That hand sunk straight into the tar golem's face. Now, all three of the creature's upper limbs were glued to the doll. The mountain troll screamed in rage, yanking his arms this way and that, pulling the doll to and fro as he struggled. But the more he did, the more he seemed to be trapped.

The cuegle roared and sunk his teeth into the tar golem's neck, ravaging it. Or, at least, that was his apparent intention— but not the end result. The creature's roars became muffled shouts, then mewling cries as he realized his mouth was stuck.

I had to stifle a chuckle at the sight of it all.

The confused look in the cuegle's eyes spoke first of frustration, then desperation. Then realization dawned there, and he raised one leg in the air in order to place a foot firmly on the golem's belly. No surprise, that foot became stuck as well.

Then the cuegle teetered, lost his footing, and tumbled over the ledge. I got a momentary case of the giggles, which took me a minute to get under control. Once I'd wiped the tears from my eyes and composed myself, I turned to face the dark wizard.

"I hate to say this, Crowley, but I've missed working with you."

"The feeling is mutual, Belladonna." He turned toward the cleft above. "Come, the way is clear."

We crept cautiously to the entrance, unsure of whether there were other guardians present. Fortunately, there were none, and we slipped inside the cave unnoticed. The interior was lit with torches, and we followed what appeared to be the main cavern without seeing or hearing another being.

"How long until that cuegle gets free?" I asked.

"Maybe fifteen or twenty minutes. We'll need to deal with it again, on the way out."

I frowned. "Should have put a bullet in its head and burned it. Too late now." I paused and listened, focusing on the caves ahead. "Shit, someone's coming. Hide us!"

Crowley looked around. "It's too open here, and there's too much light. We'll stand out like a sore thumb." He pointed at a small side tunnel, high up the wall. I assumed it was a ventilation shaft. "There—I'll boost you up."

I shook my head. "No need."

I ran at the wall, wall-walking halfway up until I was high enough to grab the ledge. The footsteps were getting closer, and I heard voices as well. I pulled myself up, and Crowley used his shadow limbs as he followed close behind.

We hid in Crowley's shadow camouflage up in our high perch, and observed the scene below. It wasn't just a small party coming our way, but a seemingly endless procession of creatures. Short, squat duende came first, in crude leather armor and carrying weapons of roughly-wrought iron and bronze. Then followed other creatures: spiders the size of German shepherds; fish-men with bulging eyes, frog mouths, and gills on their necks; *guajonas* in dark cloaks, blood-sucking witches with vulture's legs and feet and taloned hands; tiny *trasgu* carrying wooden pikes tipped with long spear points made of flint; and finally, the mouros.

The mouros were the lords of this underground territory, anyone could see that. They were glorious, in a way, and reminiscent of the fae back in the States. Tall, beautiful, and almost effeminate in their features and mannerisms—yet they moved with a predatory grace. They wore burnished bronze armor and crested helms, and each carried a long bronze sword at their hip.

I motioned for Crowley to follow me back down the shaft. "They're marching to war against us." I pulled out my cell phone, but I had zero bars this far underground. "Damn it!"

"We can't go back that way, that's for certain. Too much traffic, and we'll be discovered in minutes. I'd say our only course of action is to find this Piscina and steal it away, before the Ojáncanu's army overruns your villa."

"By the way, did you see him down there? He's hard to miss.

A ten-foot-tall cyclops with long red hair and six fingers and toes on each hand and foot."

Crowley shook his head. "I did not. Perhaps he's pulling up the rear of the formation?"

I pursed my lips and exhaled forcefully. "One could hope. C'mon, let's see where this tunnel leads."

21

The ventilation tunnel wound and twisted a few hundred feet, then angled up sharply. Since we could see daylight above, we backtracked until we found a small side tunnel that was large enough to explore. It was more like a crack in the wall, really, but it was the only other path of escape.

We squeezed through the crack, noting that it angled down and not up. That was something, at least. Hopefully it would exit into another tunnel and provide us with a way around the Oján-canu's army.

The crevice narrowed significantly the farther we went. I turned sideways and continued until I got stuck. Or, rather, until my hips got stuck.

"Crowley, I can't move. You're going to have to pull me out."

"Can you see anything ahead? It's going to be difficult from this position to pull you, but I think I can lodge my shoulders in and push you through."

I took a moment to calm myself and take in my surroundings. Crowley's faint mage-light spell illuminated enough of the way ahead for me to see that it did open up beyond this choke point. And beyond that, I saw what might have been the flicker of torchlight playing off the walls.

"I think there's an opening ahead. Alright, push me through —but if you cop a feel you'll regret it."

"I'll use my feet, then." Crowley placed both boots on my rear and pushed. "Be advised, this might require a bit more force than I anticipated. Your behind, while quite lovely, is also firmly wedged in this cleft. A moment, please."

"I swear, if you make one comment about how your hips are narrower than mine, I'll punch you in the throat."

A smile tugged at the corners of the wizard's lips, but he maintained his composure, saving himself from an ass-kicking. "I wouldn't dream of it. Now, inhale, please."

He pushed with his feet while extending two shadow tendrils past me. They anchored into the walls and latched onto my hands, pulling me while Crowley pushed from behind. The shadow limbs felt like slick mist on my skin at first, but when they latched on they felt like oily, squishy octopus tentacles... or snakes. Even with my upbringing, it creeped me out.

When I finally popped through, Crowley's "assistance" flung me forward, and I nearly tumbled out of the opening ahead. My upper body hung out and over the end of the crevice. The only thing that saved me was my tactical belt, which snagged on the lip.

Slightly disoriented, I hung there for a moment and took in the scene below.

Shit-piss-fucking-hell.

I felt Crowley's hands on my ankles as he began to pull me back. I wiggled side to side to assist him, remaining on my belly as I verified what I'd seen.

Yep, there was a *culebre* down there, along with all its treasure. I saw piles of gold coins and bars in stacks, silver goblets and platters, gilded weapons, and gemstones in glittering piles.

All the pretty things that dragonkind loved to collect. Culebre were winged serpents, related to dragons but lacking limbs and the ability to breathe fire. This one must have been old, because it was huge—easily fifty feet from nose to tail. Its wings, while massive, were wrinkled and showed the signs of many battles.

I saw something else below, chained to the wall amid all that treasure. Every so often it would move, making its chains jingle —but it was too small, and we were too far up to see it clearly.

Crowley laid down beside me to see what I was looking at, and in the close confines of the crevice his body pressed firmly against mine. The guy just didn't give up.

"Well, that certainly presents a conundrum," he said. "Are you familiar with this breed?"

"Culebre. Yeah, we've run into some smaller ones over the years."

"Do you think we can sneak past it?"

"Only one way to find out." I picked up a pebble and tossed it below. It pinged off a piece of plate mail inlaid with gold and gems. While the culebre never stirred, the thing it had chained to the wall stood up and began to glow.

Now, I could make it out clearly. It was a sprite, probably captured by the dragon for its beauty and resemblance to something shiny and valuable. Poor creature—no telling how long it had been down there.

"We have to rescue it," I said.

Crowley inhaled sharply. "Belladonna, this is no time to be taking in strays. Might I remind you that we have a mission to complete?"

I pushed myself to my feet. "I'm fully aware of that. Call this a tactical decision, then—because if that faery has been down there for any length of time, it's heard things. I'd bet bullets to beers that it knows where we can find the Piscina."

Crowley sat up and regarded me for several seconds. "Very well, it is your op. How shall we proceed?"

"Can you lower me down there using your shadow thingies?"

"Can a unicorn defecate rainbows? Just tell me where to set you down."

"As close to the sprite and as far away from the culebre as possible."

He nodded. "Consider it done. I will remain up here to pull you out if something goes wrong."

"Uh-uh, that's a bad idea. Serpents can squeeze through some pretty narrow gaps, and I'm pretty sure this crevice is how that thing gets out to go hunting. Look, there's an exit on the far side of the cavern. Think you can cause a cave-in if we need one?"

"It will be dangerous, but yes."

"Okay then. Lower me down, and wait for my signal."

22

True to his word, Crowley lowered me to a spot on the far side of the cavern, nearer to the sprite than the culebre. Once I got to firm ground, I crouched and remained still for several seconds to make certain the beast was still asleep. *Still snoozing. Let's hope it stays that way.*

I crept across the cave, careful to avoid disturbing the drake's treasure. It was probably spelled, and the culebre would likely be alerted just as soon as anyone touched it. I didn't want the thing to wake until we were ready to split the scene, so I tiptoed between stacks of coins and piles of gemstones as I made my way to the sprite.

She was a pitiful-looking thing—dirty, thin, and dressed in rags. But she was also beautiful, and she shone with an ethereal light that was breathtaking and mesmerizing. No more than a foot tall, she was built like a miniature ballerina—all grace and potential energy. She had bright green eyes, long golden hair, high cheekbones, and lips that seemed to hold a permanent pout.

I snuck within a few feet of her, and the faery held a finger to her lips. "Speak softly. The culebre is accustomed to my voice, but unfamiliar sounds may wake it."

"I'm Belladona."

"Oh, what a pretty name! And it suits you. Deadly and beautiful, you are, that's plain to see." She paused and wrung her tiny hands together. "Are you here to rescue poor little Kiara?"

I nodded and pointed at her chains. They were iron, of course, and impervious to her magic. The shackle around her ankle had caused her skin to break out in weeping sores, even though she'd stuffed rags between her skin and the cuff.

"You know what I'm going to offer—a favor for a favor. Your freedom for your help." The truth was, I'd free her anyway, but I needed to work out a bargain first to ensure that we'd receive her help. She was fae, after all, and there was no guarantee that my assistance would be returned in kind.

"I can't help you take any of the serpent's treasure. It's cursed, and she'd wake and tear us to shreds before any of it left her cavern."

"That's not what I'm here for, and I wouldn't free you just to see you captured again. What I need instead is information."

The little fae's face brightened. "A quest! Are you here to rescue a princess?"

"What? No."

The pout that played on her lips became more pronounced. "A prince, then?"

"Nope. Sorry to disappoint, but my prince is far away and safe."

The little sprite crossed her arms and stuck out her lower lip as she plopped down on a lacquered jewelry box. "Boo! If there's no romance involved, it's no fun."

I thought for a moment, then raised a finger in the air. "Well... my companion is only helping me because he has a crush on me. Does that count?"

She looked up at the opening high above from which I had descended. "I suppose. But he has a darkness about him which speaks of tragedy and loss. I don't see how you two could ever be an item—but then again, all the great love stories are tragedies." She rubbed her tiny chin and narrowed her eyes. "Fine then, I'll help you if you free me. Tell me of what you seek."

"We're here to steal the Piscina de Cristal from the Ojáncanu. Can you tell us where it is?"

She nodded enthusiastically. "Not only can I tell you where it is—I can lead you to it. As it so happens, the Ojáncanu has something of mine in his vault." She stood and turned around, pointing a thumb over her shoulder at her back. "See? No wings. The Ojáncanu stole them from me, just to be cruel. Then he gave me to the culebre, knowing I wouldn't be able to escape."

"So, you'll help us?"

"Only if you can get us out of here alive... and help me retrieve my wings. I could grow more, but it took me ages to get the color just right. *Morpho meneleus* blue is terribly hard to emulate."

"I think we can manage that," I said with a smile. I signaled to Crowley to come down, and he descended the wall on shadowy spider legs that sprouted from his back.

"He's creepy, but kind of cute—even with the burns," the sprite whispered.

"Yeah, but he's a bit of a pig," I replied.

"All the pretty ones are," she said.

I smiled. "Not all of them."

Crowley lowered himself down next to us. "Who's a pretty pig?"

I rubbed my temple. "Never mind that—we were just having a little girl talk. Now, we need to bust our new friend Kiara out of here and cause a cave-in to keep the culebre from following us. Can you do it?"

"Of course." He looked at the sprite. "After I free you, how much time will we have to escape?"

Kiara pinched her chin between her finger and thumb and frowned. "Not long. Once, a duende stumbled in here and tried to steal some gold. He didn't make it far."

Crowley turned to me. "Get ready to grab her and run." He sprouted eight shadow arms, and grasped the faery's shackle with two of them.

I nodded. "Do it."

The shackle popped with a metallic clink, and I immediately snagged up the sprite and ran for the exit. I heard a hissing roar, and glanced back to see the culebre slithering after a shadow figure, up the wall and into the crack we'd entered by. Crowley followed right behind me. After we were out of the culebre's lair, he collapsed the cave behind us.

"Think that'll hold her?" I asked.

"For a while, I think." He admired his handiwork. "But we'd best get the Piscina and be on our way before my shadow construct runs out of steam and the culebre learns she's been taken."

I set the sprite on the ground. "Hopefully we can be in and out long before then. Lead the way, Kiara."

23

Kiara led us down tunnel after tunnel, always seemingly just ahead or just behind any mouros, duende, or other minions of the Ojáncanu that were wandering the same areas. We slipped several patrols, thanks to the faery's uncanny knack for sensing danger and avoiding it. But as we went deeper into the mountain, our near run-ins grew less frequent. Soon, we traveled the tunnels undisturbed.

"Are we nearly there?" I asked the sprite.

"Close. In fact, from here on we should be as quiet as possible. The Ojáncanu's vault directly connects to his throne room far above by a hidden staircase. He's known to wander down there for hours on end, admiring his many treasures."

I arched an eyebrow. "Just curious, Kiara—how do you know all this?"

She held up a hand, signaling that we should wait, then crept up to a nearby tunnel intersection and glanced left and right before responding. "In answer to your question, I know the Ojáncanu's habits because I was his lover, for a time."

Crowley did a double-take. "Say what? Just how does that work, exac—"

I backhanded him in the gut, cutting him off before he offended our guide. "I take it you didn't end things on the best of terms?"

Kiara shook her head. "He cheated on me with a nymph, so I cut his ear off."

"And that's why he took your wings and gave you to the culebre." I checked my weapons and did an ammo count in my head as we continued down the tunnel. "Do you think he'll be in his throne room, or with his troops?"

She shook her head. "He fears the Anjana, Daughter of the Serpent. Even though her power is diminished at the moment, she's still a formidable foe. No, he'll be hiding and waiting for news of the outcome of their attack."

"How'd you know who I was?"

"You may not have your mother's height, but you do share her beauty. Jacinta Becerra is known to the fae who dwell in these lands."

Crowley cleared his throat. "Kiara, you don't mind if the Anjana gains possession of the Piscina?"

"Mind? After what the Ojáncanu did to me? If I could, I'd help you carry it out of here." She cocked her head to listen for a moment, then waved for us to follow as she took off down the tunnel. "Come now, it's not far."

Kiara led us to a massive arched doorway that had been cut from the rock, easily over ten feet tall. It was intricately carved with runes and symbols in a language I didn't recognize. An iron-bound door guarded the entrance to the Ojáncanu's vault.

The sprite patted an exposed area of wood on the door, just above the iron kickplate that was riveted to the base. "This is it: the Ojáncanu's treasure room."

"Any idea how to open it?" I asked her.

"Don't look at me—I thought that was what you brought the wizard for," she replied.

Crowley crossed his arms and studied the door. "Give me a moment." He rubbed his chin, then reached out, running his hands just above the surface of the door and archway—inch by agonizing inch.

"If you could hurry this up, that would be great," I said. "I don't much like the idea of running into that culebre on the way out of here."

The wizard ignored me as he continued to examine the door. Then, he closed his eyes and began chanting as he twisted his hands and fingers into impossible patterns. Soon, threads of shadow drifted from his hands to the doorway, where they filled the runes and carvings in the arch and door. As the shadow filled the clefts and crevices that had been carved into the door, I noticed that the outlines and patterns it followed altered slightly from the original.

Crowley kept muttering and gesturing as the patterns covering the door and frame were filled and altered, one by one. Within moments I heard a click, followed by the sounds of gears turning and deadbolts unlocking. Crowley stopped chanting, then he opened his eyes and pushed on the door. It swung inward on well-oiled hinges, opening to reveal a long stone hallway lit by torchlight beyond.

"Time to get this over with," I said as I stepped into the tunnel.

"Wait!" Kiara yelped, too late. As I shifted my weight forward, the flagstone I'd stepped on depressed with the ominous sound of stone scraping on stone.

Crowley grabbed my jacket and pulled me back, just as a number of darts shot out of the wall into the space I'd been occupying a split-second prior.

"It's trapped," Kiara said.

I glared at the sprite. "You might have mentioned that before Crowley opened the door."

She raised her hands and shrugged. "Sue me, already. I figured you'd assume it was rigged, what with this being a treasure room in a cavernous dungeon and all."

Crowley tilted his head and pursed his lips. "She does have a point, you know."

I covered my face and groaned. "In the future, when raiding a giant's underground treasure trove, I'll make sure to be more careful. Now that we've established that I'm no Indiana Jones, can we get on with this? Crowley, do me a favor and trigger the rest of the traps."

24

H is voice oozed with smugness as he replied. "Your wish is my command. Allow me." Dozens of shadow tendrils erupted from his hands. The smoky cords of magic and aether shot forward into the tunnel, pressing on each flagstone in the floor to reveal any surprises that lay ahead.

The variety of traps that the Ojáncanu had installed were impressive. Fire shot from jets in the walls, spikes extended from the floor and ceiling, massive ax blades swung across the hall, and a green noxious gas seeped from between the cracks in the wall. Not every flagstone triggered a trap, but Crowley marked the ones that did by leaving shadow residue on those stones.

We waited for the gas to dissipate, then gingerly stepped over the trigger stones as we made our way to the treasure vault. As we entered the vault, I couldn't help but gasp in astonishment and amusement. The place was an obsessive-compulsive's wet dream.

Everywhere I looked, treasures were neatly organized into stacks, bins, and boxes, each labeled and tagged in meticulous handwritten script. Not a single coin was out of place, and despite the size of the vault, every spot and corner was free from dust, cobwebs, and mold—stuff you'd normally see collecting inside a monster's treasure stash.

"Wow. I'd say your ex has issues, Kiara."

She batted her eyes and frowned. "He's a bit—how do you humans say it? Anal retentive?"

"That's just a shrink's polite way of calling someone an asshole," I replied. "Speaking of which, grab your wings and take us to the Piscina so we can get out of here before the big fella shows up."

"Too late," Crowley croaked from nearby.

My head snapped in the direction of his voice. He was dangling in the air with a huge, six-fingered, disembodied hand wrapped around his neck. The dark wizard sprouted spikes and spines made of shadow from every surface of his body, piercing the hand and causing the Ojáncanu to toss him away. Crowley bounced off a nearby stone column before landing in a heap on the floor, dazed and temporarily out of commission.

The rest of the giant's body coalesced into view, and he was a sight. The Ojáncanu was nearly as tall as the door we'd entered through, and almost as broad, with muscles rippling across his arms and bare chest. He wore a leather kilt, similar to the *pteruges* that Roman soldiers had once worn. It was belted at his waist by a wide, three-buckled leather kidney belt that covered most of his abdomen.

His chest and arms were bare, save for the thick leather bracers at his wrists, and his skin was covered with scars and coarse red hair that matched that on his head. His head was shaved around the sides, and the remaining shock of bright red hair above his single, massive, unblinking eye had been woven into several long braids that reached his waist. He nearly dropped his huge bronze-headed spear as he shook out his hand and sucked at his fingertips.

The giant roared and cursed in ancient Galician. I understood him clearly, since I'd been raised speaking the modern and ancient dialects of that language.

"Fucking wizards! Always full of tricks. Should've burned the lot of them, back during the Dark Ages." He eyed the wizard through narrowed eyes. "A bit scrawny, I suppose—but certainly meat enough to flavor a stew."

I whispered in a sidebar to Kiara. "Psst... any ideas?"

"Um, run?" she replied. Then she took off at a sprint, scrambling along the wall and over to a small, ornate chest. The sprite reached inside the keyhole and rooted around until it clicked. She flipped open the lid and pulled out a lovely pair of butterfly wings colored in shades of cerulean blue and bordered in black.

"My wings!" she declared, hugging them to her chest.

"Kiara, you'd better not bail on us," I whispered loudly, just as she reached over her shoulders with surprising flexibility to attach her wings. Interestingly, they snapped into place and sort of melded with her shoulder blades, just as if they'd been there all along.

The sprite flapped her wings a few times, then snapped them forcefully as she leapt into the air. Soon, she hovered gracefully, wings beating a steady tempo as she floated in midair. She looked back over her shoulder, admiring her wings at work as she flew in twists and loops.

"Wheeeeee!" she sang as she flitted around the room, heading in a circuitous manner toward another arched doorway at the back of the vault. The opening revealed a spiral stairway beyond, which I assumed connected the treasure room with the giant's throne room many levels above us.

"Kiara, we had a deal!" I shouted, not caring if the cyclops noticed me or not.

"I'll be right back!" she sang in her high-pitched voice. "Don't die while I'm gone, alright?"

"Damn it!" I cursed as I reached under my jacket to pull the

Uzis from their shoulder rigs. The giant had nearly reached Crowley, who still hadn't quite recovered. I had no doubts about the Ojáncanu's intentions; the cyclops was licking his lips.

"Maybe I'll just take a bite from his leg," the giant mumbled, fully engrossed by the many meal prospects that Crowley apparently presented. "Just to see how tender he is. Then I'll know how long I'll need to let the stew simmer."

"Hey, ugly!" I yelled, flipping the submachine guns to full auto and depressing the triggers. I fired in short bursts, wanting to conserve my ammo, and a dozen or so rounds slammed into the giant's back.

He roared and stamped his foot, shaking the ground a bit. "What's stinging me?" he yelled, slapping and swiping at his back as if the bullets were nothing more than ant bites.

Shockingly, that was about all the effect they appeared to have on the giant. My jaw dropped as he brushed away several flattened bullets from where they'd hit his bare flesh. The bullets left small circular welts on his skin, but otherwise they'd done zero damage.

"Well, that's just peachy," I muttered.

Then I charged the cyclops, screaming like a banshee at the top of my lungs.

25

I was halfway across the treasure vault and nowhere near my goal of taking the Ojáncanu's attention off Crowley. The fact was, this was one stupid giant. Sure, he was pissed at finding us in his treasure room, but after Crowley had done his porcupine routine, the giant had zeroed in on him to the exclusion of everyone else in the room.

Namely, me.

The Ojáncanu had shaken off the pain of the "bee stings" I'd caused with my Uzi submachine guns, and he was only a few steps away from Crowley. Apparently, he perceived me as being of little consequence—no surprise, considering my stature and complete failure at causing him damage. Or, he was saving me for an after-dinner snack.

The cyclops hummed a silly tune to himself as he sauntered over to the wizard. "Stomp his bones and tear his flesh, cook eggs and hash with the bloody mess..." Or something to that effect. I was moving at a flat-out sprint, but there was no way I'd get there in time to save Crowley... and I had no idea how I'd save him from the jolly red-haired cannibalistic giant, anyway.

Then, something captured my attention as I whizzed past. It

looked like a bird bath, with a shallow bowl and pedestal cut from the purest crystal, clear and flawless without a single crack or blemish. In the center of the shallow receptacle on top, a pool of shimmering, glowing liquid pulsed and vibrated in time with each step the giant made.

The Piscina. Now, I'd have some leverage over the giant. I just hoped it'd be enough to get us out of here alive.

I skidded to a stop and drew both my Desert Eagle magnums, firing them in the air. The Uzi machine guns were suppressed, so they hadn't made much noise. But I didn't have silencers on my Desert Eagles, and the .44 magnum rounds were loud as hell in this enclosed space. Plus, I was much closer to the giant and Crowley than I'd been—so the noise immediately got a reaction from the Ojáncanu. He hunched his massive shoulders and began ponderously turning in my direction.

Just to ensure I had his complete attention, I decided to taunt him. "Hey, dipshit! Yeah, you—the giant redhead who's so ugly, he has to sneak up on his mirror. You're so ugly, I bet your mother had to be drunk to breastfeed you. You're so ugly, I bet you had to trick or treat by phone when you were a kid!"

He'd fully turned to face me by this point, and looked like he was getting pissed. "What did you say about my mother?"

Hah, found his weakness. "I said, your mother is so ugly, she makes blind kids cry. She's so ugly, your family took her to the zoo and they thanked you for bringing back the escaped baboon. She's so ugly, you took her to the circus, and they offered her a permanent position in their freak show. She's so ugly..."

The giant held up one of his huge, six-fingered hands and cut me off. "I get it. Everyone knows my mother is ugly. It's a point of pride among female cyclops. Now, be quiet while I tenderize this wizard. I'll get to you in a minute."

The giant began to turn back to Crowley, so I fired a round

into the stone floor next to his magic bird bath. He turned back around immediately.

"Got your attention now? Back away from, my friend, or I'll shatter the Piscina de Cristal into a million pieces." I fired another round that ricocheted off the flagstones, narrowly missing the Piscina.

The Ojáncanu's eye swung back and forth between me and the Piscina de Cristal. Then, he looked at me and squinted. "You're one of the Anjana's bitches." He leaned toward me and took a long sniff. "No magic. Either she rejected you, or you're still a whelp."

"I may not have any magic, but I have a pair of boomsticks that'll turn the Piscina to dust. Then what will you do?" I asked.

"You wouldn't," he replied. "She needs the magic, just as badly as I do."

I scowled. "Are you serious? I can't stand that witch, and I've been doing everything I can to get out from under her."

"Join me, then. I'm in need of a new concubine."

I screwed my face up into a look of disgust. "Um, no. Just... no." Crowley was beginning to stir behind him, so I decided to keep him occupied by stringing him along. "But, just in case I was interested..." I pointed the barrel of one of my pistols at his groin and moved it around like a laser pointer.

"How does it work?" He laughed. "It works just fine, believe me."

Ugh. Men. They're all the same. "Yeah, but I like 'em big, if you know what I mean. Meaning, I'd like to see the merchandise, before I commit to anything."

The cyclops' face split into a wicked grin. "Well then, let me show you what you're in for as my concubine."

He reached down and lifted his leather kilt—and wouldn't you know it, he wore it like a Scotsman. Totally commando. I resisted the urge to barf.

"Hmmm... looks a little small to me."

The giant's face lit up with indignation. "Small? I'll show you small..."

He grabbed his manhood with one hand and lifted it for me to see, just like I figured he would. Males were so easily manipulated. All you had to do was hint that they might get laid, and they'd do the stupidest shit.

Thanks for playing into my hands, dickweed, I thought.

Then I shot him three times, right in the cock and balls.

Based on what I'd seen nine-millimeter rounds do to the skin on his back, I figured I had little chance of causing him permanent injury. But a .44 magnum packed a serious punch, and I figured it'd hurt just like getting racked. Turns out I was right, because the Ojáncanu's eye opened wide, and he made a little squeaking noise as he grabbed his sack with both hands and fell to the floor.

26

"Crowley, get up. We have to go, now!"

The wizard wobbled to his feet, then staggered around the giant—who was preoccupied with writhing on the floor in pain.

"Grab the Piscina, and let's go," I hissed at Crowley as I grabbed his hand, pulling him along beside me.

He reached out with his free hand toward the magic bird bath, but nothing happened. I slowed to allow him to concentrate fully on the task. Still, nothing occurred—except that Crowley tossed his cookies, all over the vault floor.

"I can't seem to cast any magic," he said between heaves.

"You have a concussion. Great." A quick glance at the giant told me he wouldn't be down for long. "C'mon, it's time for the backup plan. Can you walk out of here?"

He nodded. "I believe so, yes."

"Alright. Just be sure to stick close, because it might get hairy on our way out."

I ran over and picked up the Piscina. For a three-foot tall crystal sculpture filled to the rim with magic, it was exceptionally light, if awkward to carry. The trick would be carrying it out without spilling any of its magic. I had no idea what would happen if I did, but I figured it couldn't be good.

I carefully heel-toed it toward the giant's private entrance, because I figured it was the easiest and fastest way out. "Let's go, Crowley."

I lodged the door to the stairwell shut with a giant chair before ascending the stairs. I figured it wouldn't hold long against the cyclops' size and strength, but it'd at least slow him down.

When we got to the top landing, I could already hear the giant banging on the door below. It was made of thick wood, and banded with iron like the one we'd entered through. I gave him just minutes before he busted through it.

Crowley leaned against the door frame of the entrance to the Ojáncanu's throne room. "You're looking a little green around the gills there, Crowley," I said as I carefully set the Piscina down. "Give me a minute to do some recon."

He waved me off with a flick of his fingers, resting his head against the cool surface of the stone wall. I slowly cracked open the door to the throne room, peeking through the opening to see what we were up against.

What I saw shocked me. There were bodies strewn everywhere—mouros, duende, giant spiders, and trasgu alike. None had been spared from the destruction, and from the looks of it, the attack had happened just moments prior.

A loud crash and a roar of anger and pain from below told me that the Ojáncanu had broken through. I grabbed the Piscina and pulled Crowley upright.

"Come on, we need to get moving." I threw open the door, and we scuttled through as quickly as possible.

"What happened here?" Crowley asked as we skirted around pools of blood and twisted bodies.

"I have no idea, but I'm not going to look a gift slaughter in the mouth. Considering how many stairs we climbed, we should be close to the exit. Let's just hope it's clear the whole way out, and that we don't run into whatever did this."

We exited the throne room and kept heading up and out of the cave system, but with every step it seemed that the Ojáncanu was getting closer. He was obviously still in a lot of pain and moving slow, but he was gaining on us. We simply couldn't move that quickly while I carried the Piscina and Crowley was concussed. Plus, the piles of bodies lying everywhere often presented obstacles to our escape.

We were almost to the exit when Kiara flitted into view. "There you are! And I see you found the Piscina. Told you I would fulfill my end of the bargain."

I set the Piscina down and glared at her. "We did, no thanks to you."

Her tiny face crinkled into a frown. "Did I not lead you to the vault?"

I rolled my eyes and glanced over my shoulder. "Look, we can discuss this later. Right now, we need to move. Your ex is right on our tails."

The sprite smiled maniacally, an expression that was somehow fitting on her cute pixie face. "Oh, don't worry about him—I have that covered. Now, all we have to do is hide for a few moments and allow him to pass us by."

I was skeptical, what with her bailing on us in the vault. But I complied when Kiara led us to an alcove, and Crowley was still out of commission and just along for the ride anyway. I watched as Kiara dipped a finger into the Piscina. She licked the magic that clung to her finger like cake frosting and made a face that spoke of pure ecstasy. I guessed that ingesting raw magic was a rare treat for a faery, so I couldn't hold it against her—but the noises that came from her made me uncomfortable.

After Kiara was done making sexy-time sounds and faces,

she cast a spell over us, one that I assumed would hide us from the Ojáncanu. After that, we waited.

Not long after, the Ojáncanu walked right by us, muttering curses in ancient Galician and modern Spanish and holding his nut sack in one hand. I fought back a laugh as he tottered by, guarding his man parts to keep them from getting bumped by his thighs. It had almost been worth the trouble. Almost.

I opened my mouth to speak, but Kiara placed a finger to her lips and shook her head. Then she held up one hand with her fingers spread, and began to silently count down to one by folding each finger in turn. On cue, we heard a roar from the mouth of the cavern—then a lot of yelling, then a great deal of crashing and thrashing around.

Eventually, the noise faded off into the distance. Kiara smiled and dropped the illusion. "I believe it's safe to leave now," she said.

"Kiara, what exactly did you do?"

The sprite placed a finger on her chin and smiled coyly. "What, little old me? I simply found the culebre and told her that the Ojáncanu had a change of heart regarding our disagreement, and he had finally freed me from her clutches."

"At which point she rampaged through the caverns, killing everyone in sight," I replied.

Crowley spoke up from where he leaned against the wall a few feet away. "I hope you're not complaining. Now, can we please get back to the villa, so I can succumb to this head injury in peace?"

EPILOGUE

Two days later, Crowley and I enjoyed some much-needed rest and relaxation at Playa Rodas on the Illas Cíes. My family owned a small getaway in Vigo, the ownership of which dated back centuries. We had taken the ferry to the islands, along with a cooler full of food and beverages, and had spent the better part of the day lounging on the beach.

Crowley had been taking selfies of us the entire time. Although I'd finally figured out what he was up to, I decided to let him have his fun... if only because I knew that Colin would be sweating it back home.

Petty, I know, but a girl has to keep her man in line.

We'd taken the Piscina de Cristal back to the Anjana, and true to her word the old bitty had agreed to allow me to return to the States for a period of no more than ten years. What she didn't know, and what I didn't tell her, was that I'd taken a flask of that liquified, concentrated magic with me. Eventually, I'd find a way to use it to break free from the Anjana's influence.

Unfortunately, I'd also accidentally spilled some of the Piscina's magic on myself while escaping the Ojáncanu's cave.

Crowley stretched languidly on a towel next to me. He'd

managed to hide most of his scars with a pair of Ray-Bans and a boonie hat. It made him look like a total tourist... but it was also kind of cute. And despite the scars on his hand and arm, he'd gotten a few looks from passersbys already, probably due to his olive skin and rippling abs.

I wasn't jealous—much. My man was back home, waiting. I kept thinking about what I was going to do to him when we got back, and it involved a lot of ripped clothing, popped buttons, and messed up sheets.

Something on my chest caught the sun, flashing brightly with reflected light. I quickly pulled my bikini up to hide it, but not before Crowley noticed.

He rolled onto his elbow and lowered his shades. "How do you think he'll take it?"

"Not at all, because I'm not telling him," I replied, adjusting to a more comfortable position.

"And you don't think he's going to notice that you're randomly breaking out in scales, all over your body?"

I shrugged. "I'll just wear long sleeves and cry 'girl stuff' if he wants to get busy at an inopportune time." I sipped on my drink and smirked. "Besides, that boy is putty in my hands. Trust me, he'll never be the wiser."

Crowley laid back on his beach mat and towel, adjusting his hat so it shaded his face. "The druid's not half as dumb as he looks, and not one-tenth as clueless as everyone thinks. So far, he's outsmarted me, a two-thousand-year-old necromancer, a Norse demigod, and more than one member of the Celtic pantheon. I give it a month before he figures it out."

I considered his words. "He won't find out. And I'll tell him when I'm damned good and ready."

"So be it," he replied. "And, Belladonna... did I ever mention how much I love snakes?"

THE VIGIL

Note to readers: This story also takes place after *Underground Druid*. Again, there are a lot of spoilers in this short story. If you haven't read Book 4 in the Colin McCool series yet, you might want to read it before you dive into this tale or *Serpent's Daughter*.

27

I was headed to Stewart Island, which was pretty much the southernmost part of inhabited New Zealand, from what I'd gathered. Well, unless you wanted to go to the Auckland Islands —but apparently there wasn't much there but some rocks and birds.

Hemi's mother had summoned me, more or less.

Actually, Maureen had gotten the call—a cryptic message from a woman with a Kiwi accent. She'd said that if the druid didn't bring her son's body home soon, she'd come to retrieve it herself... and then there'd be hell to pay. Maureen had seemed to think that the reference to hell was literal, and she'd booked me a flight right away, following the instructions the lady had left with her.

The actual flight had "only" been twenty-eight hours, but once I landed in Dunedin, an old Maori man—who described himself as Hemi's uncle—intercepted me. He shuttled me, along with Hemi's coffin, onto a rickety old puddle-jumper of an airplane that looked like it'd been built circa World War II. I was pretty sure I saw a faded RAF logo on the fuselage, but decided it was best to avoid asking questions—ignorance being bliss and what-not. It rained like Noah's holiday the entire way, with thunder, lightning, and turbulence that resulted in a bone-jarring, white-knuckled flight. Somehow, we landed safely in Bluff, a small town on the southernmost tip of New Zealand's south island.

I asked the old man why he wasn't flying me all the way to Stewart Island. "Oh, one of my nephews will take you the rest of the way. He's a fisherman, and his dad pretty much runs things off shore around here. They'll see you and Hemi safely to his mother, don't you worry."

Soon after that, a skinny young Maori who looked to be just past his teen years pulled up in a rusted white Toyota pickup truck. He jumped out and extended a hand in greeting. "You must be my cousin's best mate. Pleased to meet you, Colin—heard a lot about you. Just call me Eek—everyone does, yeah?"

Eek wore flip-flops, floral board shorts, and a pink wifebeater. He loaded Hemi's coffin into the back of the truck by himself. Again, I didn't ask questions. He drove us to a pier where we approached a boat that was little more than a skiff—a sight that certainly gave me pause. As I recalled from the maps I'd looked at, it was a good twenty miles from Bluff to Stewart Island.

"We're going on the open seas... in that," I said, pointing at the skiff.

"No worries, mate. It'll get us there. Trust me, she's seen a lot more ocean than most sea-liners." The kid clapped me on the shoulder and began untying the boat. I figured it couldn't be worse than the plane ride I'd had with his uncle. I shrugged, hopped aboard, and made myself as comfortable as possible.

A few minutes into the boat ride, I drifted off to sleep. I dreamed that Eek had gills in his neck, webbed hands, and fins for ears, and that we were riding on the back of a huge sperm whale. I woke up a few hours later, alone with Hemi's coffin and my Craneskin Bag on a rickety dock in front of an old shack. It was nearly night, and light from within the shack revealed a woman bustling about the place. I smelled food, and while the smells were unfamiliar, they made my mouth water.

I heard a voice come from the shack. "Ah, he's awake. Drag my son's coffin in here, and then you can eat."

I did as she asked, struggling a great deal more with the coffin than Eek had when he'd loaded it into the truck and boat. Pulling it through the sand was no small feat, but somehow I got it inside, scraping it across the concrete floor of the shack. The single room inside was sparsely furnished, with just a small bed in the corner, a tiny table with two chairs, a counter with a sink and a portable stove, a few cabinets, and some shelves that served as the pantry.

The lady who'd identified herself as Hemi's mother fussed at the stove. Soon, she hustled me to the table and brought me a plate of food. She'd heaped it with some kind of purple tuber, steamed fish, and a piece of fried bread that looked and smelled delicious.

"Eat," she commanded. "You have a long night ahead of you."

I waited for her to sit, then took a seat across from her. "Mrs. Waara..."

"I am not Mrs. Waara. Not by a long shot. Hemi's father and my husband are two very different men."

"Then what should I call you?"

She tilted her head with a shrug. "Call me Henny. You'd never get my full name right, anyway. Now, eat—your food is getting cold."

I dug into the food she'd prepared. The simple meal was filling and satisfying, especially after the long trip I'd had. I'd only nibbled at my meals in flight. The gravity of my task had eaten at me and affected my appetite.

I'd brought my friend's body home to his mother, and it was my fault that he was dead.

After I finished my meal, Hemi's mother took my plate and washed it in a basin, then she left it on the counter to dry. I spent some time looking at her while she worked, taking measure of the woman Hemi had held in such awe.

Henny's face was classically Maori—with high cheekbones, a broad but feminine nose, full lips, perfect white teeth... and a glare that could scratch glass, despite her good looks. Her eyes were brown, and her skin tone was lighter than Hemi's. I would have described it as almost ashen, if I'd had to assign it a color. She was tall and slender, but not willowy—being strong through the shoulders and hips. That much was plain to see, even in the full-length skirt and oversized t-shirt she wore. Her hair was long, frizzy, and thick, and it draped loosely about her shoulders.

She was barefoot, and her feet, while well-cared for, reflected a lifetime spent walking in touch with the earth. She wore no jewelry, yet she was as regal and composed as anyone I'd ever met or seen. Henny was no common woman, for sure— although I wasn't quite certain *what* she was, exactly. I had my suspicions, based on comments Hemi had dropped and what I'd seen since I'd landed in Dunedin.

After she was finished cleaning, she sat across from me again and pulled out a pack of Dunhills, offering me one before lighting up and taking a long, slow drag. She exhaled smoke through her nostrils, making herself look a bit like a dragoness, with her deep-set almond eyes and the lizard-like way she regarded me—almost like a bug she was considering for an evening snack.

Henny pointed her cigarette at me and tsked. "I almost killed you, you know, when Eek left you on the dock." She took another pull from her cigarette, and the cherry glowed bright-orange in the fading light inside the hut. "But I need you. Eek's not strong enough to do what has to be done. And Uncle Tay... well... he doesn't want to get involved."

She puffed again and nodded. "But you'll do."

28

"I'm happy to help out, any way I can. But if you don't mind me asking, what exactly do you need me to do?"

She set her cigarette in an ashtray on the table and folded her legs under her on the chair. "You took too long to return him to me. So, I have to go home to bring him back."

I was eager to respond with an apology, and blurted out the rehearsed speech I'd practiced over and over on the trip over. "I'm sorry—deeply sorry—for your loss. Hemi is... *was* my dearest friend, and..." Suddenly, something she'd said registered. "You said, 'bring him back.' I don't believe I fully understand."

"Back. From the dead. What's so hard to understand about that, eh?" She puffed at her cigarette and scratched her cheek. "Wouldn't have been such a chore, had you brought him here straightaway. If his spirit was still clinging to his body, I might be able to bring him back quick, no problem. But now..."

"You can bring him back?"

"That's what I said, didn't I?"

I choked back a sob. "You're kidding, right?"

"Why would I joke about something like this, the life of my

own son?" Tears ran down my cheeks, and she scowled. "Oh, don't go all soft on me now. Hemi said you were the sentimental type. But I need you hard as stone and sharp as shark's teeth right now. Understood?"

I nodded and got my emotions under control. "I apologize that I took so long to bring him to you. I was recovering, you see."

She waved my explanation away and frowned. "Excuses won't placate a mother's anger—not when they come from her children, and certainly not those given by their playmates. But what's done is done. As I said, I have to go home, and that's a long way from here. And while I'm gone, you're going to guard Hemi's body."

"Okay... but from what?"

"Whiro's going to come for him, sometime tonight. He wants to eat Hemi's body, to make himself strong and break out of his prison in the House of Death."

"Whiro, the god of darkness and evil?" She nodded as she pulled on that cancer stick again. "And just how am I supposed to stop *him*?"

Henny flicked ash from her cigarette and replied in a haze of exhaled smoke. "Your magic will confuse him, because it's foreign to him. It should hold him off until I get back."

"Um, Mrs.—er, Henny—I don't know if Hemi told you anything about me, but I don't have much magic."

She snorted. "He did, and he was right about you—you underestimate your own potential. Trust me when I say you can hold Whiro off until I return."

I rubbed my forehead and sighed. "Correct me if I'm wrong, but if he's imprisoned, doesn't that mean he can't come for Hemi?"

"Parts of him can—pieces of his power. And, he has many, many who serve him."

"Great." She arched an eyebrow at me, and I held my hands up in surrender. "Don't worry, I'll do what you ask." I glanced over to Hemi's coffin. "I owe him that much."

She nodded. "And more. Now, let me have a look at my boy." She stood and walked over to the coffin, removing the straps that held it closed and opening it with little fanfare. "Hmmm... the old *tangata nui* did a good job of knitting him back together— although I can see where his magic did its work."

Henny fussed with Hemi's corpse, touching him here and there. She didn't seem at all affected by the fact that she was looking at her deceased child.

"Ah, this is interesting." She crooked a finger at me. "Come here, druid. It seems your benefactor has left something for you."

I stood and walked over to the coffin, hesitant to see my friend's body. I still wasn't good with his death, even after learning there was a chance to bring him back. But when I brought my eyes up to look at him, he looked peaceful, like he was just resting. It was as though he might wake up any minute.

Henny leaned over him and reached into his chest. Not above, but *into*—as in, her hand went incorporeal and through his breastbone. She dug around inside and pulled something out, something misty and not altogether solid. It was dull grey, but it glowed bright silver by the time she pulled it completely free from Hemi's body.

"Here, *pākehā*, you're going to need this." She slapped her hand against my chest, and fire filled my body. Then, I passed out.

"YOU SURE DO SLEEP A LOT." Henny closed the lid on the coffin just as I woke on the floor of the shack. I sat up and took stock of my current condition. "Feel better?" she asked.

Surprisingly, I did. Much, much better. "What *was* that?"

She smirked. "Looks like the old giant wants you to experience what it'll be like, once you come into your full power. That's how it always works, you know, with deities. We tease you with a taste of power, then you dance to the songs we sing."

"Yes, I'm familiar with the custom... Great Woman of the Night."

Henny sniffed as she regarded me with hooded eyes. "Figured it out, did you? You're not as dumb as you look."

"I try my best to avoid being just another pretty face."

She squatted and grabbed me by the chin, turning my head left and right as she examined me. "Eh, so maybe you're not. It's just as well. You'll need your wits about you when Whiro shows up." She stood and placed her hands on her hips. "Well, are you just going to sit there? You need to get ready. As soon as I leave, they're going to come."

I pulled myself to my feet. "Right... so, I guess wards would be the first order of the day?"

She hissed at me and glowered. "How am I supposed to know how your magic works? Just get it done, and don't let them take my boy. Because if you do, I *will* kill you... no matter how much my son likes you."

Henny was serious. As the Maori goddess of night and death, I knew she could easily end my existence. I gulped and nodded. "Consider it done."

29

Threats and decrees delivered, Henny disappeared in a whirlwind of shadows—one that apparently served as a portal to wherever she needed to go.

"Crowley would love to meet you," I mumbled as she vanished into a cloud of darkness and mist.

Presumably she'd gone to the underworld, or what served as such for the Maori pantheon. Why she couldn't just summon her own son's spirit from the place she ruled was a mystery, and I hadn't thought to ask her about it. She'd made it sound as though it was a long journey—and since she didn't seem to care for me much, I hadn't asked questions.

Deities were weird, in my experience. They were mortal in that they could be killed, but immortal in the sense that they'd always come back eventually. Some demigods were the same way, and apparently Hemi was one of them. Thus far, I'd deduced that his mother was one of the more powerful members of the Maori pantheon—and I suspected his father was human.

Hine-nui-te-pō had been married to her father, Tāne, before she knew him as such. According to the legends I'd read, she'd rejected the incestuous creep and ran away to the underworld. There, she'd taken up residence as the ruling deity in order to keep Tāne at bay. Thus, it followed that Tāne was not Hemi's father. It also followed that, although Tāne was Whiro's immortal enemy, he would not intervene on Hemi's behalf.

That meant I was on my own here.

I started with what I knew—that Whiro was the embodiment of darkness, sickness, and evil. I'd read that he commanded evil spirits, and Henny had said he had followers, which I assumed would be humans who worshipped him. So, I'd need to be ready to repel spirit-based creatures, and to fight off mortals who'd most certainly try to steal Hemi's body for their master.

The floor of the hut was concrete, a fact for which I was grateful, because creating wards in dirt, sand, or on a wood plank floor would have been problematic. I grabbed some permanent markers from my Craneskin Bag and warded the place completely, certain to create an iron-clad circle of magical protection around Hemi's casket. I also wrote wards into the door frame, threshold, and lintel, around the windows, and even into the walls. I hoped like hell that Hemi's mom wouldn't be pissed that I'd written all over her house. But I figured she could afford to buy another one, being a powerful Maori deity and all.

When I activated the wards, I noticed something peculiar. Henny had hinted that the Dagda had wanted to give me a taste of my full potential. I'd never considered myself to have any particular aptitude for magic, but then again, I'd never really applied myself. Over the previous weeks, I'd been studying with Finnegas in earnest—partially because I wanted to learn healing magic, to prevent what had happened to Hemi from happening to anyone else I cared about.

But I was also studying with him because I knew I'd royally fucked myself when I'd double-crossed Maeve. Eventually, that bill would come due. If I wasn't prepared for it, I'd be a goner. So, after regaining my strength I'd spent hours every day reading, taking lessons from the old man, and practicing new and improved spells I'd learned.

That still wasn't enough to cause the effects I felt when I activated my wards. For expediency I'd linked them all, so I'd only have to activate them once. Activating a ward took time, so by setting them up this way it significantly cut down on the amount of prep time I needed. The only downside was that I'd have zero protection until I was completely finished—but it was a calculated risk.

When I slapped my hand down on the connecting link, imbuing it with power to activate the entire network of protection, I felt a rush of power flow out of me like nothing I'd ever felt before. I'd already activated my second sight, and what I saw had me gaping, because my wards absolutely *pulsed* with power —far beyond any protections or spells I'd managed to create prior to receiving the Dagda's "gift."

"Whoa. Now that is something," I exclaimed, looking at Hemi's casket as I spoke. "I wish you could see this, buddy. You'd be impressed."

By the time I finished activating my wards and admiring my handiwork, I sensed visitors were already on the way. How I sensed them was another interesting quandary. It was like I was connected to the earth, plants, wildlife, and even the air around me. The connection was subtle, but telling—because when the first wave of Whiro's flunkies arrived, I felt them coming.

They had the entire hut surrounded, in a cordon that was roughly fifty yards out and closing in fast. With one last check to ensure my wards were solid, I reached into my Craneskin Bag and grabbed my battle gear. I strapped on my tactical belt—the one that carried my Glock and holster—my new favorite sword, spare magazines, and a few other surprises I'd whipped up while I'd been recovering.

I threw a motorcycle jacket on over that, thankful for the relatively cool weather on the island. The jacket was reinforced with Kevlar, and it would provide some additional protection. Finally, I grabbed my war club from the Bag, spinning it like a cane before I flipped it up to rest on my shoulder.

"Alright, buddy," I said to Hemi's casket. "Let's see who or what your uncle Whiro sent us."

30

The first wave was made up of humans. And just how did I figure that out? I stepped outside the hut, looking to face the first bunch of whatever showed up head on. Seconds later, the sounds of bullets whizzing past my head greeted me—along with repeated muzzle flashes appearing in the surrounding darkness.

"Fuck!" I ducked back around the door. "Whatever happened to attacking with clubs, swords, and spears?" I muttered.

A hail of bullets rained down on the little hut. While I was concerned for my own safety, I was even more worried they'd do enough damage to the structure to break my wards. The wards were only viable so long as the underlying surface they were written on stayed intact. Sure, if I'd expected gunfire, I might have imbued them with protection against physical attacks... but I honestly hadn't expected it.

Shit. Well, two could play that game. I reached into one of the pouches on my tac belt and pulled out an improvised grenade. Druid magic worked by amplifying and redirecting forces found in nature. That was good, considering it meant I wasn't really reliant on any particular power source—not like the fae or most wizards were. However, as Finnegas had been teaching me recently, it also meant you had to have something to work with in order to perform druid magic.

In this case, I'd taken an M84 flashbang grenade, the type military and SWAT teams used, and enhanced it with a little druidry. I'd also glued double-ought shotgun pellets around the casing for a little extra shock and awe. If my calculations were correct, the thing would go off like a frag grenade. I pulled the pin, activated the spell on it, and tossed it out the door.

The results were unexpected, to say the least. I'd tossed the grenade as far away as possible, roughly forty feet from the hut. However, the blast and subsequent shockwave rattled the windows in the hut, and it also peppered the door frame and walls with pellets. Not enough to break my wards, mind you— but if it had been closer, it might have caused complications.

Note to self, develop directionally channeled fragmentation grenades for future use.

A loud shockwave of sonic energy, light, and heat also resulted from the blast. While I was protected by the wards I'd placed on the hut, the goons outside shooting at me weren't so lucky. Those within ten feet of the blast were shredded, and anyone within twenty-five feet or so was knocked unconscious or had their eyes fried shut. Everyone else in that first wave of attackers had been affected, too. Most held their heads, screaming as blood and fluid poured from their eardrums, noses, and mouths.

After that, it was mostly clean-up. I picked them off one at a time from within the relative safety of the hut. Was it sporting? Hell no. But necessary? You bet. I'd counted more than a dozen of them, and they wanted to feed my best friend's corpse to their crazy, creepy, flesh-eating deity. *Uh-uh. Not on my watch, freaks.*

I'd repelled the first attack. I checked my phone and cursed, because it'd barely been an hour since Hemi's mother had vanished. I had no idea how long it would take her to retrieve his spirit or when she'd be back, so I assumed I was in for a long night, just as she'd said.

Quiet fell over the surrounding forest and nearby beach for a few blessed minutes after that. I listened to the sound of the surf as I reloaded magazines and reinforced my wards. It was almost peaceful—except for the moans of a few wounded I'd been unable to locate in the trees and bushes farther out. I had a feeling their master would take care of them, once he made his appearance.

Minutes later, I heard a splashing sound coming from the beach. The hut was in plain view of the shore, so I glanced out to catch a glimpse of what was coming in the moonlight.

"You have to be fucking kidding me," I hissed. Huge, tentacled limbs with suckers the size of saucers were pulling something big up over the dock. A bulbous, purplish-red body surfaced behind the writhing mass of thick, muscular appendages. One dinner plate-sized eye blinked and stared at me as it pulled its bulk on shore.

The massive arthropod slowly dragged itself closer to the hut, up the short stretch of land to where Hemi's body was ensconced inside my wards. While I knew the wards would hold against most anything magical or supernatural, the hut itself wouldn't stand a chance against this beast. With limbs as thick as telephone poles and a body the size of a Volkswagen Beetle, I didn't think I'd have much chance of preventing it from pulling Hemi into the deep once it reached us.

I emptied the Glock into it, but I may as well have been throwing rocks. I tossed another supercharged flashbang at it, and while that seemed to have some effect, the result wasn't nearly as impressive as it had been with the humans. What else did I have at my disposal that might deter a giant octopus?

I had a flaming sword on my hip, but as of yet I hadn't tested its effects and limitations to any real extent. Besides that, one swipe from a single tentacle and I'd be fish food. I had my war club, but that presented the same tactical challenges. I could throw a firebomb at it, but I didn't have any prepared—nor did I have anything at hand with which to make it.

I looked up at the clouds in the distance, and thought back to my flight from Dunedin earlier. *I wonder... can I really do it?* Only one way to find out.

I extended my senses outward, up into the air above. Miles away in the troposphere, I saw lightning flash within grey clouds over the mainland. That's what I wanted to tap into.

At first, all I felt was the wind as it played about overhead, tossing and turning this way and that—like a playful child rolling in a pile of raked leaves. I reached farther still, past the clear skies above and toward the storms I'd experienced earlier, seeking to use the potential energy created by the meeting of warm and cold air and the multitude of microcollisions between ice crystals and water droplets in the sky.

While I worked, the octopus got closer. As it did, I noticed a foul odor of rot and death coming off it in waves. The stench was partly due to necromancy, and partly due to decomposition. Knowing that it wasn't a living creature any longer made me feel better about frying it—so that was a plus. The downside was that if I could smell it, the damned thing was close enough to do me in for good. *Colin McCool Killed By Zombie Octopus*, the headlines would read, if I didn't make a connection with that great big battery in the sky.

Finally, I felt it, like a faint buzzing or vibration in the air currents on high. Once I felt it, I *pulled* on it with my will. *Here*, I said in my mind. *Land here.*

And it did.

31

The cloud discharged its energy, reaching from miles away to ground itself in the enormous mass of dead flesh and muscle that was about to squeeze the tiny hut into splinters. At the last minute, I jumped up on a wooden chair—just in case I didn't have complete control over the direction of the spell. As the lightning made contact with the flesh of the creature, I felt it run through the octopus and into the ground beneath.

One billion volts of electricity fried nerve tissue, muscle, and fat alike inside the creature, short-circuiting its nervous system and turning it into a quivering heap. Rotten flesh sizzled and burned for a few moments, then its eyeballs burst, splashing the sides of the hut and ground with fermented aqueous humor.

The absolute reek of burnt, rotting octopus flesh was nearly unbearable—and despite having seen a number of atrocities in my short lifetime, I vomited all over my boots. The dry heaving continued for a minute or more, until my olfactory nerves became deadened to the smell. Finally, the necromantic spell dispersed, and the beast deliquesced into great pools of runny flesh and liquid that slowly flowed back into the sea.

A sibilant, hissing voice spoke from the still darkness outside the hut.

"It was s-so very hard to animate that creature. What a shame. But you are an amusing human, druid. Tell me, do you enjoy eating pineapple, or perhaps coconut?"

It was Whiro, or one of his human servants. But I doubted any human necromancer could animate that octopus, so I was betting on it being the evil deity of darkness himself.

"Whiro, I presume?"

"So they call me. Come outside and join me, so we might speak face to face."

His voice was like dry leaves rubbing across snakeskin—creepy, hypnotic, and strangely soothing. With every syllable, I felt more and more congenial to his suggestion that I exit the hut. A part of me thought that Whiro seemed downright friendly, all things considered.

Thankfully, I'd felt this sort of magic before, back in Fuamnach's castle—so I immediately recognized his ploy. I resisted the compulsion he'd cast over me with an effort of pure will, along with a flash of the Dagda's magic that I cast just outside the door. The spell was crude and instinctually executed, but it made the shadows outside the hut recede and fray around the edges like charred paper.

Whiro hissed, and his voice shrank back along with the shadows. "That was... unpleasant, and rather rude, but I will let it slide. Now, in answer to my question?"

"If you're going to ask me out for piña coladas, let me just say right up front that I don't swing that way. However, I could set you up with a couple of vampires I know."

A wheezing chuckle came from the shadows. "Oh, but you are a cheeky one. I only ask because I enjoy the flavor, and I was hoping I might get you to partake before I eat you."

A coconut and a pineapple flew through the open door and

into the hut. The dim light cast by the single bulb overhead revealed both to be crawling with grey worms and huge, thumb-sized maggots. I kicked them both back out the door, and in my mind reached out to the storm again. If this evil fucker thought he was going to eat me, he had another thing coming.

Just as I sensed a flicker of energy in the clouds over the mainland, something cut the connection like a hand flicking a light switch off.

"Tsk-tsk, druid. No fair getting my brother involved. Tāwhir-imātea agreed to stay out of this, once he'd handed you and my nephew off to Ikatere. He's always had a soft spot for Hine-Nui-Te-Po, but he is loath to incite my anger." Whiro coughed with a wet rattling noise that made my stomach turn.

He's not well... lucky me. I wondered if I could work that to my advantage.

As the Maori personification of evil continued speaking, his voice tickled the edges of my resolve. "Now, if you would just step outside for a moment, we can skip a great deal of unpleas-antness and save you a good deal of pain."

I fought off the compulsion a second time and willed myself to respond. "I have a better idea—why don't you come in and get me?"

"Have it your way, then."

Soft, rolling footsteps echoed from outside. I took a peek and regretted it. All I saw was a man-shaped shadow, but it emanated evil and sickness. Fear gripped me as soon as I laid eyes on Whiro's... body? Projection? Spirit? Whatever it was, it wore malice and ill will like a cloak.

I ducked back inside the hut and leaned against the wall, squeezing my eyes shut and willing the memory of what I'd just witnessed to flee from my mind. It was no use; I was frozen with fright. As his footsteps grew closer, the anxiety and despair I felt increased until they crushed me, suffocating me with the unbearable weight of abject, illogical terror.

He spoke from the other side of the wall. "Just remember, I offered you an easy way out—"

Whiro was cut off mid-sentence, and his words trailed away in a cry of pain and confusion as a loud thunderclap and a bright flash of light exploded just outside the doorway. After the flash of light receded, I forced my eyes open in time to see that the runes and glyphs I'd written in the wood around the door had flared up in a bright silver glow. Slowly, the oppressive presence of fear and dread receded.

I was nervous, scared, and I really had to take a piss. As usual, I coped by being a smart-ass.

"So, you're not coming in after all? Disappointed!" I roared at the ceiling, doing my best Kevin Sorbo imitation. Screaming actually helped calm me, and I did my best to make my voice seem calm and collected as I continued. "I was so looking forward to those piña coladas."

Whiro's voice reflected both pain and strain as he replied. "Hine-Nui-Te-Po always was a crafty one. She knew what she was doing, leaving you to hold vigil over my nephew's corpse. Your magic certainly is foreign to me, but the night is far from over. I have plenty of time to figure it out. And if not, I have other ways to overcome you than brute force."

"Give it your best shot, cupcake. I'm not going anywhere."

I tried not to gulp too loudly as I wondered how long my wards would hold out against evil personified.

32

Whiro stalked around the hut for a few hours, probing the defenses I'd devised as he tried to unravel my wards. Every so often, I'd have to shore up a knot here or a junction there—but for the most part, they held. It made me thankful that I'd paid attention back when Finnegas had taught me about wards. Even as a stupid, wet-behind-the-ears kid, I'd seen the utility in knowing how to make and break wards.

Funny how seemingly innocuous decisions could end up saving your life.

After a time, silence fell over the hut, and Whiro's attacks and probes stopped. I sat atop Hemi's coffin, sipping some warm lemon soda I'd found as I contemplated Whiro's next move. Was he gathering his energy for a more concerted effort? Or had he given up and moved on?

"Yeah, fat fucking chance of that," I whispered as I patted Hemi's casket. "You're just too much juicy meat to pass up, buddy." I paused and considered what had just tumbled out of my mouth. "Um, that came out all fucked up. But you have to admit, if you were scrawnier, we might not be in this mess."

Just then, I felt something happening outside, beyond the

barrier of my wards. It had been a mostly clear, moonlit night on the island, but the moonlight seemed to recede as the light dimmed inside the structure. I glanced out the doorway, and saw absolutely nothing. It was as if a blanket of darkness had enveloped the tiny hut, cutting me off from the outside.

Then, with a fizz and a pop, the lightbulb overhead blew out, leaving me in total darkness. The fact that I was sitting on top of a coffin, with the embodiment of pure evil only footsteps away, did not escape my attention.

I drew the sword from the scabbard at my hip. I'd found it in the depths of my Craneskin Bag, during those long weeks after Maeve had abandoned me to starve and rot deep below ground. The sword had been something of a salvation to me while I'd been locked away, as it had been my only source of light. Currently useless as a weapon against Whiro, it could at least serve me in that same capacity now.

As the blade flared, the dancing tongues of fire that licked up and down its length illuminated the room, revealing why Whiro had chosen to cast me into darkness. There were now *other* things with me, inside the room. They were dark, ethereal things that must have been knit out of some shadowy ephemera, because I knew they were there, but they didn't seem quite real. Faces appeared at random intervals within the crowd of figures that had gathered around Hemi and me.

The faces represented people I knew, or had known. As soon as I focused in on one of them, a scene coalesced before me. It was one I knew so very well, because I'd replayed it over and over again during the weeks since his death. Shades of grey and black took form, then shape, color, and light—morphing into reality before my eyes.

In a way, it was more real than being there the first time. I saw Hemi being pulled off the mountain cliff in Underhill, and watched him tumble off into the mists until he disappeared. My heart broke with remorse and guilt, because I'd been too late to save him.

Once he'd fallen completely out of sight, the scene reset, and events played out all over again. This time I was *on* the cliff, and not climbing up when he fell. As the giant's hand clamped on his leg, I dove to catch him but missed. I slid across the rocky ledge just in time to see him tumble down the mountainside. With every revolution of his body, with every inevitable kiss of gravity and inertia, something broke, twisted, or shattered. This time, there were no mists obscuring the view. I watched with sharp detail and utter clarity as his body slammed into the ground hundreds of feet below me.

The scene played out again and again—dozens, maybe hundreds, of times. Each time a small detail changed, whether it was my proximity when he fell, or how the giant grabbed him, or the look on his face, or the manner in which his body shattered as he plummeted. And in every single instance, I failed to save him.

Just when I thought I couldn't take any more, the scene faded into darkness. The sword was still in my hand, burning a molten scar into the concrete floor. It was dangerously close to damaging the circle of protection I'd drawn around the coffin. I flipped it around and thrust the tip in the ground, out of the way, keeping a grip on it so it would stay lit. Just then, I needed the comfort of firelight. Without it, I feared I might go mad.

"I know what you're doing. It won't work," I whispered.

"That remains to be seen," Whiro's voice teased.

The shadow things swirled and reformed again, and another scene appeared around me. I was back in the cavern, trying desperately to save Belladonna's life. Blood seeped out from around my fingers, and nothing I did could staunch the flow. What remained of her life spread out in a warm pool of red around us, soaking into the dust and rock of the cavern floor.

Her heart stopped, and the scene reset.

Next, I was fighting off the dead, battling in vain to keep them from dragging her away from me. Rotting hands and fingers grabbed at her from everywhere. I shot, kicked, cut, and clawed at them, breaking and severing limbs—only to find that two more took the place of each one I dislodged.

Belladonna's face was a mask of absolute revulsion and fear. "Don't let them take me," she whispered. A ghoul lapped at her wound, and I shot it in the head. Dead, flaccid arms and hands grabbed me from behind, pulling me away from Bells and preventing me from saving her. I held onto her hand as long as possible, but she slipped from my grasp. Her eyes accused me as she was consumed alive, just a few feet away from where I watched helplessly.

Thousands of times I experienced the pain of letting her die, and each time it drove a knife into my heart. But somewhere inside that madness and chaos, I remembered that she hadn't died. We'd saved her—me, the trolls, and Finnegas.

And I laughed because I knew that somewhere, somehow, Belladonna was alive and well. I came back to reality immediately, draped across Hemi's coffin with a death grip on the sword's hilt.

"Told you it wouldn't work," I croaked.

"There's more pain there to tap," the evil one replied. "A deeper wound, one that's pure and true in all its festering misery. Let's reopen that one, shall we?"

"I wouldn't do that if I were you," I whispered. *Game fucking on, bitch.*

33

I knew where Whiro would take me next—to the cave where Jesse and I had faced the Caoranach. It was the place where I'd first suffered my *ríastrad*, my so-called "warp-spasm." This was the place where I'd killed Jesse in a mindless rage that had been triggered by the demon's overwhelming attack and a very close brush with death. How many times had I wished it had been me who had died, and Jesse who had lived?

Every detail was as clear and real as the day it had happened. The damp cool of the cave, the acrid smell of guano and musky scent of dragon nearby, Jesse's perfume and her soft, warm lips on mine just before we entered the cave. The rough feel of the cave wall as I paused, leaning on the rock as I strained my senses, because something just was not right.

There were bones strewn about, both human and animal— some old and dry, while others still had bits and pieces of rotting flesh attached. There was a presence there, of something old that was better left undisturbed. But we ignored it, because our intelligence had said that the Caoranach had only recently physically reincorporated, after having been slain many centuries earlier by Saint Patrick—who'd apparently gotten cozy with my ancestor Oisín and gotten wise to the world beneath.

At any rate, we were expecting a cakewalk. What we got was a massacre.

I experienced the quiet as we crept deeper into the cave, sensed the gnawing sense of anxiety the farther we went, and saw the looming shadow of the demonic dragoness as eighty feet of scales, teeth, and talons cut off our only path of escape. I felt her claws pierce my abdomen as she pinned me to the floor of the cavern, and smelled her fetid breath as it caressed my face, warm and scented of death and decay.

Somewhere nearby, a foreign sensation brushed the far reaches of my awareness. Whiro was living the memory with me. Was that... lust? Admiration? Respect? I couldn't be sure, but he was gushing over the Caoranach, that was for sure—and it was enough to remind me why he was making a mistake by bringing me here, to relive this memory.

The demon's claws raked my body and face, and hot blood splashed the floor and walls of the cave. She trampled me, once, twice, three times, with enough force to break my spine—but not enough to kill me. Yet. She wanted to save me, and make me watch while she tortured and killed Jesse.

One swat from her talons and my love was tossed against the wall with a sickening crunch. She fell to the floor, blessedly senseless. I screamed and raged as I attempted to drag myself along the floor using my arms alone, because my legs weren't responding to my brain's demands. Inch by inch I dragged myself along, all the while witnessing the Caoranach savage Jesse, feeling my life seep out onto the cavern floor beneath me.

The dragoness used her talons like scalpels, slicing away bits and pieces of the love of my life, then tossing them into the air to snap them up in her massive jaws. How she could even derive any gustatory pleasure from such a minuscule piece of flesh was beyond me—but I realized she fed on pain and terror, not flesh and blood.

I heard Whiro's coughing cackle come from somewhere close by. He was as yet unaware of what was about to happen.

"Man, but you are so fucked," I whispered.

That's when the dam inside me broke, and my Hyde-side was loosed from his cage. I felt the transformation come over me, and in this instance, it wasn't going to happen in half measures. This time, in this place, it was happening for real.

I didn't even fight it. Instead, I just let my other side take over. But before I gave up control completely, I "called" for Balor's Eye, inviting it to the party. Then, figuratively speaking, I sat back and enjoyed the show.

That other side of me emerged as he always did, in a near-instantaneous malformation of flesh and bone that transformed me into something large, misshapen, and not altogether human. Fomorians were the bane of the ancient Celtic world, the boogeymen who lived under the bed, the terrors that stalked the night. For all their power and magic, even the Tuatha Dé Danann feared them.

Between the magic that the Dagda had temporarily imbued me with, and the Fomorian shifter magic of my ríastrad, I had a feeling Whiro was in for quite a shock. As my Hyde-side took over, and as my body shifted into a massive, nine-foot-tall cross between Quasimodo and King Kong, the imagery around us faded away and the cabin came back into focus around us.

Don't break the building, I thought, hoping he'd hear me and listen. Thankfully, he must have heard, because instead of busting down a wall we tore out the front door and ran into the rainforest outside the hut. All around us, shadows blanketed the trees and vegetation in a manner that was highly unnatural and altogether *wrong*.

Was Whiro hiding while he made his escape?

Somewhere deeper inland, we sensed a presence retreating under the cover of night. I'd been right! Whiro didn't know precisely *what* he'd set loose, but one thing was clear: he didn't want any part of it.

My alter-ego swiveled his head in the direction of the fleeing figure, and spoke a single word. "Burn."

It would be my pleasure, the Eye replied.

34

Hours later, just as the first rays of dawn crept up to the east where the ocean met the sky, I sat outside the hut sipping L&P and contemplating the mess we'd made of the forest around me. The Eye's magic had vaporized great swaths of trees and vegetation in multiple directions. And where the rainforest hadn't been vaporized, tree trunks had been knocked over, the ground had been gouged and disturbed in every imaginable way, and small bits of liquid night pooled here and there like blood.

Because that's what it was.

I sensed a portal opening nearby, and heard footsteps approach. I stood, just in case it wasn't a friendly face approaching. Henny walked around the corner of the hut, but instead of a glare, she wore a smile across that stern face of hers. She carried a gourd wrapped in a woven net, and held one hand tightly around the neck, her thumb on the wooden stopper.

"I see you upheld your debt to my son." She walked up to me, getting well inside my personal space, and grabbed me by the shirt collar. At first, I thought she was going to kiss me, but instead she touched her forehead and nose with mine. She held me there for a moment with her eyes closed, so I closed my eyes and waited. Besides, even if I'd wanted to break free I couldn't have. She was just that strong.

After several uncomfortable moments, she released me and stepped back. "Now, tell me of all you have seen and done while protecting my son. He will want to know these things when he awakens."

"Um... don't you want to... you know... replace his spirit?"

She laughed, and while it was a pleasant sound, it had a fierceness to it that threw me off. "Oh, that's already been done. It seems most of the magic the old giant left for you has been spent, so it was nothing to bypass your spells and send my son's spirit back where it belongs."

I pointed at the gourd. "If Hemi's... um... back to his old self —then what's in the bottle?"

She snorted as her mouth curled into a smirk. "This? It's herbal tea, to help Hemi recover. Now, tell me what happened, and leave nothing out."

So I did, doing my best to avoid embellishing anything out of respect. Besides that, I wasn't all that proud of what I'd done. Not that Whiro hadn't had it coming—but if I'd been looking out for Hemi, he never would have died in the first place. I put that thought out of my mind while I related the night's events, and when I was done, Henny pursed her lips and nodded.

"Not bad, pākehā, not bad. Sounds like you sussed him out good. I doubt he'll show his face for a few decades, at least." She paused and scratched her chin. "But a word of caution—when he does, he'll remember the hiding you gave him. He'll want revenge."

I sighed. "It's not a normal week if I don't have some deity or immortal pissed at me."

She frowned, but the twinkle in her eye told me she wasn't angry. "Yes, Hemi told me how you like to stir things up."

I glanced back at the hut. "Is he awake?"

"Nah. He'll need some time to recover, so you won't be seeing him for a while. But you did your duty, and have earned the right to call my son your friend."

I nodded, acknowledging the compliment without looking like I was feeling my oats. "Henny, if you don't mind me asking —why'd you leave me to guard his body? Why not call one of the... Hemi's other family members instead?"

"I had intended to recruit some help for you. But once I saw the magic the old giant had left you, I knew you could handle it without any assistance. Besides that, Hemi tells me you're rudderless—adrift in your own indecision and self-doubt. You needed to experience what real power feels like—what *your* power feels like—to give you something to strive for, a purpose."

I looked off into the distance. "I've just had to deal with a lot of loss, is all. It can shake a person's confidence."

"Everybody deals with loss, druid. In many ways, how a person handles it determines their measure."

"I guess I haven't always handled it well."

"Nonsense. From what my Hemi tells me, you've handled it better than most."

I looked away, embarrassed by the praise.

"Hmph. Despite that smart-assed façade, you do have some humility. Maybe a little too much, if you don't mind me saying." I arched an eyebrow, and she smiled.

"He talks about you often, you know. He looks up to you— but more than that, he believes in you. Hemi was raised around the *atua*, and he knows a power when he sees it. Look what he sacrificed, all because he believes in you. Isn't that enough to make you want to quit messing about and do something with your life?"

I sat up and took a deep breath, letting it out slowly. "Point taken. And believe me, I'm working on it."

She narrowed her eyes and gave me a stare that could melt ice. "Well, work faster. If you get my son killed again, I'll feed you to Whiro."

"Yes, ma'am."

"Now, come inside and let me cook you something to eat before I portal you back to Texas." She poked me in the ribs, a little harder than was comfortable. "You are way too skinny. If we're going to find you a nice Maori girl, we need to fatten you up."

I realized I'd rather face Whiro again than disappoint Hemi's mom, so I followed her to the front door of the hut. She stopped abruptly at the door, and I almost ran into her backside as I skidded to a halt. Henny stood there gazing around the room, tapping her foot as she took in the damage.

"The bullet holes, I can understand... but if that's permanent marker, young man, we're going to have a serious talk."

Gulp.

This concludes Blood Circus, but you can read more adventures featuring Colin, Belladonna, and Hemi in the Colin McCool Paranormal Suspense series, available on Amazon. Click here to check the series out now!

And, be sure to read Druid Blood and Blood Scent, two additional novellas that serve as prequels to the Junkyard Druid series of novels!

Made in United States
Orlando, FL
10 February 2023

29790884R00088